Honor Bound

Wildcat Wizard Book 5

Get deals and new releases notifications first via the newsletter www.alkline.co.uk

Charming!

The two bloodsuckers charged.

Even exhausted they were fast.

But not as fast as The Hat.

My left arm went up in a defensive block as I raised my wand in my right hand and forced what pitiful will remained into the ancient wood. Mustering little more than fumes, I nonetheless sent the magic deep into the wand and the sigils flared briefly as the vampires reached me.

All that happened was a slight flaring of the tip, accompanied by a noise resembling a baby hippopotamus letting rip after too much curry. Trust me, I've witnessed the aftermath of such a thing, and it ain't a pretty sight. Now wasn't the time to be amused by such sounds though. Laughing at bodily functions is best done when you haven't got two pissed off, tired, and hungry vampires literally breathing down your neck.

"Me first," hissed the older vampire, a guy in his sixties with thinning gray hair pulled back into a straggly ponytail.

"Fine," pouted the other, much younger man, a suave kid with an expensive suit, gelled hair, and a very smackable face.

I ducked as they grabbed for me, their eagerness making their movements uncoordinated and unprofessional, but that's exactly what these two dudes were. Unprofessional. Noobs to the vampire scene, they'd probably been made several months ago, and they brought shame to their kind. They shouldn't have been out unsupervised, they shouldn't have been made at all.

As I ducked again to avoid a punch that would have sent my face right through the back of my head, I stepped back and caught my heel on the body of one of three vampires who'd already had a Hat special. Meaning, they were very dead, and none too happy about it. I wheeled backward, flailing as I struggled to keep my balance, feet catching on small lumps of concrete in the abandoned factory littered with glass, remnants of machinery, and the aftermath of debauched nights by kids with nowhere else to go.

I grabbed hold of the remains of a rusted machine and used it to get some cover, moving behind it as the two vamps spread out to come at me from either side. Man, I was so tired, and if it wasn't for the adrenaline still shunting through my flaccid veins I would have just laid down, said, "Have at it," and gone to sleep as they sucked the life out of me, or whatever it was they did.

As I tried to keep both of them in sight, I made a vow I'd made once before. To find out all I could about vampires. The time had most definitely come, as this unjust attack was uncharacteristic, not something you ever heard happen, and it was all because they were too new and unable to control their bloodlust. But nobody knew exactly how it worked, how they were made, turned, whatever it was called, how long the process took, or even what went on inside the body as you became a fully fledged vampire.

From one brief conversation the day the One, Mikalus the head vampire, had been resurrected with a little accidental help from yours truly, I'd been led to believe that to turn you had to be bitten by a vampire, then take their blood. A two-become-one type of thing, which was cozy and kinda nice in its own way, but there was a lot more to it than that, I was sure.

Distracted by my wandering thoughts, which I was prone to be at the most inopportune of times, I was almost too late to react as the young guy decided he'd had enough messing about and would simply bash my head in and feast on whatever remained.

The pipe he swung swished as it came at me fast and undoubtedly hard, and I only just ducked in time. Knowing how these things went, I stabbed out behind me with my wand, a simple length of wood that was nonetheless harder than any metal ever made or mined, and smiled as I felt contact with the old guy. He grunted in pain as the wind was knocked out of him.

The kid swung again, this time with me crouched down, and I had nowhere to go. As the pipe descended toward my head, there was no tunnel of light, no life flashing before my eyes, no thinking about all the things I'd do differently if I had another chance. I was merely annoyed, as he looked so fucking smug, and no way was I going out staring at a smart-ass kid with a stupid hairstyle and a suit that cost more than some cars.

So I let him smack me over the head.

The vibration rang down my spine, nothing more than a rather gentle and pleasant tingling, but he couldn't say the same. Grace, my hat, always had magic stored in her for just such occasions, and she wasn't even dented by the unwarranted assault. The young man reeled back, dropped the pipe, and held his arm as he screamed, eyes wide in shock and maybe fright. Things like this aren't meant to happen, and never would have in the world of citizens he came from mere months ago. I removed my hat, checked she was okay, then replaced her with a grunt as I stood and kicked out at the old guy behind me who thought he was sneaking up on me but was actually just waiting for a kick in the bollocks.

I obliged.

As he doubled over, I grabbed the pipe, swung at his head, and split his skull wide open. He dropped sideways, smacked against the lump of a machine, then crashed to the broken concrete floor, kicking up a cloud of dust that made me sneeze and would probably bring on my allergies. Brain oozed out of the long gash in his head.

My arm dropped as the pipe was seriously heavy and I had no energy left. I was remiss in doing so, no matter how tired I was, as, too late, I sensed the stale breath of the youngster right behind me.

Before I could turn, he bit down, and I wondered if vampires had to obey their masters. As if I had to do what this fucker told me, I was in for one seriously crap eternity.

Hi, I'm Arthur "The Hat" Salzman. Gangster. Wizard. A bit sleepy.

They Never Learn

"It's leather, you fuckwit," I mumbled as I reached behind, grabbed hold of the guy's jacket, and yanked him around in front of me.

Something snapped as I hauled his skinny body close and his hands went to his mouth as blood trickled down his weak chin. I smiled at the chipped tooth shining in the weak early morning light streaming in through the open factory doors and smashed sky lights.

"Hell, you are such a noob. Just because your teeth are sharp, or were, doesn't mean you can bite down through leather and suck me dry.

"Yum gomma pay," the guy mumbled, sounding like he had a mouthful of toffee.

"I'm sure I will pay, for something, some time, but you aren't gonna be around to see it."

Too tired to drag this out any longer, as I'd already been fighting this rogue group for half an hour, I stabbed out with my wand right at his Adam's apple. The wood slid in three inches deep like a spoon into jelly. He gasped and clutched at his throat, mouth forgotten, then fell over, making weird sounds and thrashing his legs about as he fitted. I watched, unmoved, as he died in a decrepit warehouse in the abandoned outskirts of a dying city in a poisoned world. The whole sorry debacle just made me sad.

These guys would have been bad people when citizens, their whole demeanor screamed trouble, being turned had just given them the power to play out their fantasies. The true vampires, the old ones, the responsible ones, like Mikalus and Ivan, those in charge, they should have known better than to ever bring such scum into their fold.

I wasn't their bloody Cleaner, I shouldn't be dealing with this crap. It shouldn't have happened and this was not how they usually acted. I'd only come to see Ivan about the new ridiculous mansion Vicky was now ensconced in, wanted a chat about it and a few other things, but I'd found Ivan's temporary headquarters abandoned. Not that he'd ever done more than set up a desk and his goons somewhere suitably ghetto to make the right impression on the lowlifes.

But he'd gone, and all I found were disgruntled vamps searching for Ivan, and maybe a little sport. He had to answer for this, explain himself. But I needed to know how this all worked, what was happening, and why these dudes had gone off the rails.

I should have called first. I could have saved myself a lot of hassle, and now I'd have to do it anyway.

Shattered, annoyed, covered in blood and gore, and wondering if vampires were comfortable enough to lie on, as I was close to sleep, I nonetheless pulled out my phone and called Ivan.

"Arthur, I was just thinking about you," said Ivan.

"And I was thinking about you. I came to the factory, but you weren't here."

"Obviously," he said, amused. "I'm here."

"Yeah, very funny. Some of your people, vampires, attacked me. Newbies, Ivan, out for blood. You losing control?"

There was a long pause, several deep breaths, until Ivan said, "I apologize. There have been incidents. I thought we'd taken care of it all. Were there six? That should be the last of them."

"Six? Um, hang on." I counted up the bodies, just in case I'd miscounted the first time. "Nope, just five of the fu—"

Something hammered into my back and the phone went flying as I slammed into the massive machine part. I whacked my head and bounced back, feeling the lump already hard like a boiled egg on my forehead. Ivan shouted my name down the phone but it was out of reach, and then a woman with wild long blond hair and a face only a mother could love, mainly because part of it was missing, screamed manically. She switched to cackling as she stomped on the phone then launched herself at me.

Her hard nails aimed right for my eyes, so I ducked down just as her claws hit my hat. The nails splintered and she shrieked in rage then began tearing at my hat and neck, gouging lines of flesh away.

I wriggled and bucked and finally managed to roll aside but she was lost to utter madness, teeth gnashing, eyes dark and distant. She was hardly human, more animal, and all she wanted was my blood. As I scrambled backward she came at me again, arms flailing, screeching and utterly beyond salvation, but strong with an animal's wild nature when in the throes of the hunt.

As she hurled herself at me, I rolled once more, and when she landed I grabbed her arm and whacked her hand down hard against a chunk of concrete. Her wrist snapped and she keened with primitive rage but I didn't pause for a moment and was on my feet and backpedaling just to catch my breath.

With her arm hanging limp, then twitching as the vampire nature repaired the damage, she got up and shambled toward me, determined. Then she was running and I was running away, but slowly, so she'd catch me. As she readied to tackle me to the ground and feast on delicious Hat blood, I spun then jabbed my wand right into her angry eye, popping the delicate orb that spurted fluid halfway up my arm. The wood penetrated her brain and before she hit concrete she was dead and my wand was very sticky.

I fell back on my bony ass and sighed.

"I hate fucking vampires."

Better Late Than Never

As I sat leaning against a graffiti-covered concrete pillar in the abandoned factory, nostrils full of the stench of foul bodily fluids oozing from corpses, I had a serious look at my life.

It was awesome.

Magic and fights and dangerous artifacts and tapping into the secrets of the universe, who could ask for more? But that wasn't what buoyed my spirits even as my head dropped and I fell asleep, it was the excitement I felt because I had another date with Candy this evening and I was going to go all out to impress. So it was with a smile on my face that I slept soundly amid the carnage of mangled bodies, twisted machinery, broken glass, and the decay of commerce long ago abandoned to the seedy underbelly of the city. To the criminals, the junkies, the desperate, and the lonely.

It suited me just fine. I was at home down in the gutter, because I understood, unlike most people, that this was where we belonged and life was real. Pretense was stripped away, and you got a sense of what was really happening in the world.

All the shiny buildings, the repetitive trudging through the rain to work every day, the commute, the money, the nice house, the car, apartments, it was all a veneer that could crack all too easily. I'd seen both sides of the divide, and most of what lay in between, and it was all the same when you got right down to it. If you were in the gutter, you wanted to get out, if you were out, you worried about falling in. Stress either way was the result.

I smiled as I dozed because none of that could touch me any more. I was the goddamn Hat and I'd waded through the filth and the scum and forged my own path. And now things were about as good as they'd ever been. Or as they'd ever get. I had my daughter, I had my home, I even owned my own hat. Plus I had a date. It was like Santa had been holding out on me and had finally decided to give me all my gifts at this late stage.

I awoke and glanced at my watch, feeling exhausted and unrested. No wonder, I'd had exactly seven minutes of sleep. Wearily, I clambered to my feet and stood waiting for the approaching car to pull up outside the factory doors.

With a final glance around, I wandered out into the bright sunshine of a brave new world. As I took in the cracked concrete and the skeletons of crumbling warehouses, and as the weeds blew in a gentle breeze and my hair tickled my neck where it hung long past my hat, I lifted my head and let the sun warm my face.

It was going to be a beautiful day. The sun was rising with a promise of heat and purity, washing away the last of the night terrors, and I had a whole day to get ready for the evening, even try to get some sleep.

First, I just had to have a chat with a vampire.

A Chat and a Drive

Ivan stepped out of the vehicle, but only after two goons had checked the area first. They were vampires, large ones, and I knew they were fairly new to the world of the undead. For one, they were mostly memorable in as much as goons can be memorable. Two, they were fine out in the daylight. I knew that the longer you were a vamp the harder it was to function during the day, especially when it was as sunny as this. Sure, it would take many years before you were truly forgettable, your features, your presence, everything about you fading from the memory of others, almost like a ghost to citizens or those who didn't know you well, and the same went for the sun thing. Ivan was struggling already, preferred the dark, but he could still cope. Just.

He still used an umbrella, although he wasn't so far gone down the rabbit hole that he made a goon hold it for him. Ivan was from the rough end of the criminal life, same as me, and there were certain things he would never do, feeling like a betrayal of his roots.

"What's going on, Ivan?" I asked as he approached and the goons stared at me from behind dark glasses.

"That's exactly what I'd like to know. You said you were coming to see me?" Ivan stepped close, and I caught a whiff of the scent that became stronger every month. A sweetness, a mustiness, the essence of the earth and the night. Of how freshly dug ground smells after a shower on a summer's day.

"Yeah, I thought you were still operating from here. Guess not."

"I moved last week, thought you knew?"

"Nope. In case you've forgotten, we haven't been in contact lately."

"How could I forget? Please, ride with me?"

"I've got my own car."

"I'll have it brought along." Ivan spoke quietly to a goon and he nodded. Reluctantly, but not wanting to have an argument as we hadn't seen each other more than once or twice since an incident with a book that saw me abruptly stop obtaining artifacts for the vamps, I handed my keys to the goon.

Inside the cool interior of the sedan, the tinted windows and bulletproof glass making me feel like I was in a luxurious coffin, Ivan and I settled down as we were driven away.

For several minutes neither of us said a word, then I broke the silence. "What was with those noobs? They jumped me, tried to eat me. This isn't the first time, either. There have been a couple of other incidents I've heard about. You losing control?"

Ivan grimaced but didn't try to avoid answering. "Mikalus tried to increase our numbers, which has worked well, but there's a limit, and some of the, ah, more recently turned find it hard not to turn a few of their own. They become wild, disconnected from the rest of us, set adrift if you like, unable to rein in the urges. It's complicated, hard to explain, but they were the last."

"I bloody hope so. It doesn't help your reputation. Bad for you, bad for Mikalus, bad for everyone."

"Tell me about it. This is a complicated business, Arthur. Being changed, turned, is no easy thing, so I recommended caution, but Mikalus is keen to... Let's just say that a few new to the fold got carried away, turned those that should not have been turned, but now it's over."

"Good. Now, about why I wanted to see you."

"Don't tell me, it's about Vicky. About the house?"

"Yeah, damn straight it is. What were you thinking? She can't live somewhere like that."

"Have you seen it?" he asked, staring at me really hard.

"Nope, not yet. She said she wanted it to be perfect. But it'll cause problems, set her up for a world of hurt."

"I don't see how. She needed a clean break, after, er..."

"After she murdered her husband in the drive because he scared her children and was a waste of fucking space?"

"Yes, exactly."

"So why not help her out with a normal house, not a bloody mansion? She'll be lost in a place that size. I've heard all about it and it will not end well. Trust me."

"Arthur, I really don't understand what you're saying. Why shouldn't my sister and my nieces have the best? They deserve it."

I sighed and tried to explain this as best I could. "I know they deserve the best. I know the girls should have everything they ever desire, but Vicky, she's complicated. She gets stressed, has issues. Giving her this much responsibility will drive her nuts, make her manic, send her spiraling. We both already know what happens when she gets wild."

"She is rather a willful one," mused Ivan.

"So you bought her a fucking mansion?"

"I thought it would be good for her, a way to have closure. I think you're overreacting. It'll be nice for us to spend more time together."

Then it hit, and I understood. Shit, this was worse than I'd thought, much worse. Vicky had been a handful and then some these last nine months, and more trouble than usual since she discovered her and Ivan were brother and sister, sharing the ability to transform monthly into scary-ass wolf-cum-dog type beasts. It didn't help that after a particularly bloody incident her reputation amongst the shifters had grown, and was now almost mythical.

After she did away with hubby, a.k.a. the Slug, she was sullen and quiet for a few weeks, focused on her girls, then became increasingly manic until she had what I guess was a full mental breakdown. She emerged several months later being prone to excessive violence, more impulsive than ever, and way too edgy.

We only did a couple of jobs then I called a halt to it all as she was a danger to herself and me. Since then, almost six months, I hadn't done a single job and had mostly kept out of trouble.

So what was Ivan's solution to his sister's woes? If my hunch was correct then he'd only gone and bought her a massive house so he could keep an eye on her and the kids by surrounding them with fucking vampires.

"Are you out of your frigging mind? What, you living there too? You got your people watching them?"

"What I do with my life is none of your concern, but yes, I have a room there. I use it only once, maybe twice a month. Mostly I visit, spend time with the girls, and yes, my people are there to keep an eye on them and to protect them."

"They're vampires," I said flatly.

"I know."

Ivan and I stared hard at each other, neither of us willing to back down. Our locked gaze was only broken when I heard a squeaky voice say, "Hello? Can you hear me?"

I glanced around to find we had pulled up outside a set of huge wrought iron gates. The driver had his window down and was leaning out to speak into an intercom.

"Hello?" Is this thing on?" came Vicky's voice.

"Just let us in," I shouted, then slumped back and glared at Ivan.

"Time you had the grand tour," he said.

We continued staring at each other as we sped up a long drive to Vicky's new home.

Swanky

The driver pulled up at the front of the house; it was bloody huge. Not a mansion as such, but a very large property sitting in several acres. It had a stunning raked gravel drive, plenty of mature trees, high hedges, lawns like football pitches, and the building itself was a delight. Understated, but elegant, with an ancient gnarled wisteria covered in long trails of perfumed lilac flowers covering half the front wall, probably planted right after the house was built several hundred years ago.

I knew for a fact that Georgian properties like this were worth a bundle, the original features, high ceilings, massive windows, and quality craftsmanship at a premium as so many houses, large or small, lacked all of these trademark qualities.

Ivan and I stood beside each other staring at the building for a while. I turned to him, questioning, and he smiled and nodded. "Nice, isn't it?"

"Sure is. Must have cost a fortune. I know Vicky had plenty of money from our work, but nowhere near enough to cover this." How did I know this? Because I would be hard pushed to afford something like this. It would cost two million at least.

We stood there a while longer, listening to the birds and the bees, the gardener, or one of the gardeners, mowing the expansive lawns, and the sound of Vicky and her girls—Tweedledum and Tweedledee, as I liked to call them as I always got them mixed up—laughing and shouting from somewhere behind the house.

"What's this all about?" I asked Ivan, knowing this wasn't just out of brotherly love and concern and so he could have a crash pad once a month.

"She's my sister."

"Come on, level with me."

"She's been through a lot, more than she deserves."

"I know all that, and I've done what I can, but this is extreme. She needs simplicity in her life, not complications. Maids and gardeners, staff, a huge place to look after, it's not good for her. She'll get stressed, she is already stressed, and it won't make her better."

"It was what she wanted. I thought it would be what she needed. And you've said all this, no need to keep repeating yourself."

I saw the doubt in his eyes, a flicker of annoyance. Vicky had probably told him this was her dream home so he'd obliged, thinking it would also be a good place for him to rest up when needed. Maybe they planned on a monthly jaunt when they shifted. Sibling bonding or something. But I knew Vicky better than he did, and this was a terrible idea.

"Vicky says a lot of things, much of it is dramatic, what she thinks she should have so people won't look at her funny. She's always been about keeping up appearances for the sake of the girls, and she won't let that go."

"I know that now, but I didn't realize how, er, extreme she is." Ivan actually shuddered. Guess he really was getting to know his sister.

"Haha, okay, I get it. Let's just see how she gets on. But I'm warning you. Do not use this to your advantage. Do not use the people working here to interfere in her life. Leave her to do her own thing. And do not," I warned, "try to turn her."

Ivan took a step back, genuinely shocked. "You think I want that for her? I would never do that. Never. Or the girls. They are my family. Do you know how important that is to me?"

"I think I do. Probably as important as family is to me. And Vicky is my family, Ivan. You understand me?"

Ivan nodded then wandered off, crunching gravel, hiding underneath his umbrella as the sun beat down. I watched for a moment, wondering what he was up to, then jogged to catch up with him. Guess I'd find out soon enough. There was no way he didn't have an ulterior motive for all this.

He wandered around to the back of the house, which was more impressive than the front. There was a huge patio area with outdoor furniture, a barbecue that probably cost more than my kitchen, another massive lawn, and a proper tennis court, which was where everyone was, prancing about with rackets and balls, shouting and laughing.

Maybe this wasn't such a bad idea after all.

Then I spied the topless, tanned young guy tending the flower beds, a face I'd seen before. It took a moment to recall where I'd seen him, then I remembered. He was one of the many beautiful young hopefuls that gave themselves to the vampires with the promise that after they had shown their devotion they would be turned.

So, Ivan had his spies, just as he'd admitted. But was it just to watch out for his sister, or was there another motive? I dismissed it as just me being paranoid. But that didn't mean the buggers weren't out to get us.

They usually were.

Nice House

The girls came running over and gave us both a hug, jabbering away about how cool their new home was and did we want to play tennis? We both declined, as there is too much shame in being beaten by children when you're gangsters.

Vicky skipped across the lawn, smiling, her ponytail bouncing like a frisky puppy let off the leash for the first time.

"Isn't it a beautiful day?" she chirped, grinning and looking, I have to admit, absolutely amazing.

"Sure is. Sorry to turn up uninvited," I apologized, as I hated it when people did that. Although hardly anyone knew where I lived, I still had the odd guest appear. Angels, elves, demons, that kind of thing. Plus vampires, always vampires.

"Mi casa, su casa. Let's go get a drink and I can show you around." Vicky gave me a peck on the cheek then gave Ivan a massive hug and said, "Thank you so much, this is perfect. The girls love it and they've already made new friends with the neighbors."

"My pleasure," said Ivan, who smirked as Vicky bounced off, her tennis skirt showing off shapely legs, her tight vest revealing a trim, lithe, more rounded figure than I'd ever known.

"Okay, I admit it, she's looking great. Maybe you did the right thing."

"Maybe," said Ivan, suddenly serious.

"What?"

"You got me thinking, is all. What if this all goes wrong and everything falls apart? Comes crashing down around us?"

I slapped him on the back and said, "Don't worry, of course it will. This is life, dude, it always goes to shit."

With happiness in my heart, because Vicky and the kids were content for now, I laughed at Ivan's frown and we followed the mad mini-mom up the garden, through the French doors, and inside.

After a tour of the house that took way longer than I'd have liked, which was any time at all, as it was typical Vicky style and taste, meaning bad, with lots of shiny things seemingly bought by a blind child with dreams of becoming a princess one day, we finally settled in what Vicky called the day room. I called it too fucking big and badly decorated.

I sat on an armchair that almost swallowed me whole, only saved by the sheer quantity of cushions, whilst Ivan took his chances on the sofa next to Vicky. Brave man.

We chatted about the new place for a while, and about what we'd all been up to the last few weeks as we'd all been involved in our own lives and me and Vicky especially hadn't spent the time together we usually did. Not that I minded the peace, the chance to recover after her and the girls living with me and basically ruining my house and my life. Then things took a turn for the dark.

We talked of Cerberus, and how the new boss, Carmichael, had taken a rather aggressive approach to all things magical. I hadn't seen him once in the intervening months, but I'd heard all about how this new boss handled things. He took no prisoners, literally. He'd eliminated a number of less than adept thieves, along with several collectors who'd refused to hand over their artifacts when his Hounds had paid them a visit.

The underground was buzzing with stories of him and his very direct, very deathy approach, and I knew it was only a matter of time, probably when I took another job, before I met him again. We had a lot of unfinished business, but I was surprised that Cerberus hadn't been on my case already.

"Excuse me a minute," I interrupted, as I spied something outside, turning away quickly before anyone saw.

"You okay?" asked Vicky.

"Just need to stretch my legs. Hip's been playing up. Give me five?"

"Sure." Vicky was too caught up in her bubble of excitement to ask questions, like since when did I have a dodgy hip?

I exited through the French doors and glanced right where the bushes were just bouncing back into place. Checking the girls were still playing tennis, I walked hurriedly around the side of the house, whipped out the wand, and forced my will, with the deadliest intent, down into my most prized possession.

As the figure of a man in blue overalls, still holding a trowel in his hand, hurried away, head down, back exposed, I let loose with the magic and a silent jolt of searing heat, burning white-hot, shot in a straight line like I had laser sights and punctured a hole right through the back of the dude.

He stopped dead in his tracks, turned to face me before his mind and body caught up with what had happened, staring from me to his chest in shock. The hit had been direct to his heart, and I could see Ivan's chauffeur through the gap in the guy's chest.

He keeled over and thudded into the neatly mown lawn.

The chauffeur ran over, saying nothing but raising an eyebrow.

"Give me a hand. Let's put him in the car."

He nodded, still silent. This was business as usual for the driver of a gangster-vampire overlord, and fair play to him, he was strong, fast, and discreet. With a nod once the body was hidden, the shorthand for so much in this gangster life, I wandered back inside, brushing a speck of blood off my jacket at the doors.

"You look better, almost glowing," said Vicky.

"Yep, all better now," I said, smiling.

Ivan stared at me curiously. His nostrils flared and he inched his head forward. I shook my head.

"So, get on with it," I said to Ivan.

"Get on with what?" asked Vicky.

"With whatever this is all about. He's hiding something, he's got an ulterior motive. He's up to something."

"Whatever makes you think that?" asked Ivan, crossing a leg to reveal black socks with Betty Boop pictures.

"Because I know you, and I know you want something. From both of us."

Vicky's eyes lit up, the thrill of danger almost brimming over.

Ivan wanted something all right, and I knew it would be epic.

I wasn't wrong.

Wiping the Slate Clean

"You owe me," said Ivan, and he meant it.

"I know." I was surprised it had taken him as long as it had to call in a favor I'd wondered if I could ever repay.

"I saved your daughter from being fed on by the vampires. Took her place, became one of them."

"Yeah, I know this. But let's not forget, you wanted this. You wanted to be part of their family. Before you knew you had a family of your own, that is."

"That changes nothing. I belong with them as much as with Vicky. But you still owe me."

"And even after all I've done for you, and for Mikalus, we still aren't even, right?"

"Right."

"Not even after I found your sister for you? All that madness that went down, the risks I took? I gave you a family, same as you kept mine safe. That's not enough?"

"That was different, and you know it.

"But after this we are done?"

"This will wipe the slate clean. We'll be even. Quits. You will owe me nothing."

"What about me? What do I do?" asked Vicky, pouting about being left out.

"You stay here and lord it up in your mansion," I said, knowing it was futile but a wizard could live in hope.

"She's involved, very involved. You two are the only ones who can do this, nobody else. Mikalus himself has given me this order, or request, whatever you want to call it."

"So, what you're saying is the original vampire, the One, has told you to tell us, in no uncertain terms, that we are to do this?"

"Exactly."

There was a stony silence as we all let that sink in. I didn't like it one bit, but there wasn't much I could do about this. Vampires had a deep sense of obligation, I did too, and Mikalus knew as well as I did that I owed Ivan a lot, and Mikalus too, for he hadn't killed us all, asked anything of me yet.

Now was the time to pay the piper, and there really wasn't a way to refuse without it being seen as a personal insult.

"Ask him then," squealed Vicky, acting like she had ants in her pants, wriggling and squirming on the sofa like she needed a wee. Maybe she did, but she was old enough to go without having to be told.

"Fine," I said with a sigh. Reluctantly, I looked at the boss of most criminal activity, at least the organized stuff, in the country, who I happened to owe a massive favor to, and for my sins I said, "Tell me."

So he did.

Selling My Soul

Half an hour later, with my head reeling, my knees feeling weak, my mind already devising devilish plans then rejecting them as I knew deep down nothing would work and this was a fool's errand, I slumped back into the chair, nearly disappearing under the weight of the cushions I'd piled all around me, probably in an attempt to get away from the madness, and said, "No fucking way."

"Remember, it will wipe the slate clean," said Ivan.

"You can let the slate stay dirty. You're out of your mind if you think this can be done. And besides, this is more than wiping the slate clean. This is a whole other level. If I did this, and I won't because I'm not a suicidal moron," I glared at Vicky as she was about to say something cheeky, "then it would mean we were way beyond even."

"You'd be rich. Richer than almost anyone else in the country. And you can get in. I know you can. Don't try to deny it."

I stared Ivan down, but I knew he must have found out. I guess it wasn't difficult. I knew I shouldn't have jumped back into his office to deliver the book last year. Once he did some checking into how that was possible and discovered the only way was with some serious fae assistance, or the way I'd done it, he'd have been convinced. He knew I owned a Teleron.

I'd stolen it from Carmichael, then used it to deliver the angel right into his lap. I wondered what had happened after, unfortunately not the death of Carmichael as he was still around, but you can't win them all.

"Fine," I said eventually. "So you know."

"Know what?" asked Vicky.

"I own a Teleron, all right?" I blurted, exasperated. "And no, you cannot, ever, use it. It's mine."

Vicky was non-plussed. "What's a Teleron?"

"If I may?" said Ivan.

"Be my guest."

"A Teleron, and there are maybe two in existence, is a small device that allows the owner to picture a place in his mind and open a portal directly to it from anywhere he, or she, may be in the world. It is a shortcut through the land of Faery, through the very Nolands itself, and Arthur here stole one from Cerberus."

"Arthur! You never told me."

"Why should I? You've been off the rails, acting mad, unstable. You think I wanted you nicking it and using it? You've been running wild every month when you change, you've been acting foolishly, the two jobs we did almost ended in disaster because you wouldn't listen, like you were brand new to this game, and besides, it's mine."

"Have I really been doing that?" asked Vicky, crestfallen.

"Yes."

"I'm afraid so, dear sister. I thought this new home might calm you down, help you to recover, but..."

"But what?" Vicky was genuinely puzzled, but then, we never see ourselves the way others do, never notice when we begin to act a little different.

"But maybe it was too much for you. This house, the staff, it may not have been the best of ideas."

Ivan was a good guy, sort of. He'd listened to what I said and thought on it. It didn't mean I would do this job though.

"But we love it here," protested Vicky.

"Let's stick to the topic at hand, shall we?" I said. "And I'm not doing it."

Ivan edged forward to avoid getting sucked in by soft furnishings, and perched on the edge. "You will have millions. Both of you. You won't owe me a thing. Plus, and I have permission from Mikalus, if you agree, and trust me, you will, then I am able to answer any questions you might have. Any."

"Any?" I asked, perking up.

"About vampires and how it works and about, er, anything?" asked Vicky.

"Yes," said Ivan with a sigh.

I mulled it over for about a millisecond, then my mouth spat out the word before I could change my mind. "Deal."

"Deal," said Vicky, although she'd wanted to do this anyway

We asked our questions.

The Truth About Vampires

"Let's start with the basics," I said, getting in first before Vicky went off on one and asked a gazillion stupid questions.

"As you wish," said Ivan.

"How do you make a vampire?"

"You must be bitten by a vampire. It begins the process, you will change. Feel the hunger. But you will not, ah, have all the benefits. You will be stronger, smarter, but you won't live longer or have true vampire powers. For that, you must take the blood of a vampire in return."

"So Mikalus wasn't lying about that," I noted.

"He doesn't lie about anything."

"Are you alive?" asked Vicky.

"Oh, definitely. Very much alive."

"Just immortal?" I asked.

"Nothing lasts for ever, Arthur, nothing. It slows the process down, but there's a limit. What that is, nobody knows. Mikalus is the eldest, the true Second almost as old as him. Maybe it will be four hundred years, maybe a thousand, who knows?"

"And you still need food?"

"Us young ones, certainly. I am led to believe that the older you get, the less normal food is required. You become more vampire, if that makes sense, over the years. Then, blood is what is required."

"How often do you need to feed?"

"Not that often. Again, the older you are..."

"And you don't kill? You don't suck your victims dry?"

"Arthur, please. Look, allow me to say this, and make it absolutely clear. Vampires are people. Different, but people. Do most people murder? No. Vampires are the same. We have a long history of willing people who gave their blood freely. It doesn't take as much as you'd think, but yes, it has to be fresh so to speak. Once a month maybe, for me. For Mikalus, it is different. He needs more, and more often."

"Wow, you weren't kidding about opening up, were you?"

"Mikalus felt this was for the best. This is private though. Never to be shared with another living soul."

"Right, here's a doozy. Mikalus, or was it you, hinted about there being a number. That there could only be so many vampires. How many is that?"

"A hundred thousand. A hundred thousand true vampires."

"Why?"

"I don't know. That's the truth. It's what I was told. I could get no further answer."

"Okay, fair enough. Now, this whole lineage thing. The further removed from being bitten by the One, the less, er, vampire you are, right?"

"Absolutely. You get the most strength, intelligence, power, by being chosen by the One. And down it goes, less and less effective. But all have extended lives, and are stronger than normal, but it becomes less obvious, yes. It's why Mikalus has given of himself. Even if you are bitten by a weak vampire, if you take the blood of a more powerful, older vampire, you will become one step removed from them. The essence of vampire, the infection if you will, is most concentrated in the One and weakens as the line descends."

"And he's going to let how many feed from him?" I asked, scared shitless that a hundred thousand vampires would descend on the city and be turned into Seconds.

"Arthur, this is information even most vampires don't know. We don't all talk on the phone and share secrets. We have very disparate groups, we have vampires who know no others, many who are content with their lives, feeding occasionally, maybe from a partner, a loved one, and they have no interest in changing. But the majority don't know or understand what the rules are. Anything else?"

"Yeah, what's with Aurelius, the angel. And Mikalus and Carmichael? They all knew each other. And Carmichael, what's the deal there? He's a magic user, he's obviously old, from around Mikalus' time, and they knew each other. What gives?"

"Oh, you're going to love this," said Ivan as he leaned forward conspiratorially. Vicky and I did the same, enchanted by the gleam in his eye. At that moment all I could think was how alike he and Vicky were. They apparently both loved to gossip, although I'd never have thought it of him.

"Tell us," gasped Vicky. She'd heard all about our meeting and was pissed she'd missed it, so this would make up for it.

"Carmichael killed Mikalus."

"What!?"

"Seriously?" asked Vicky.

I was incredulous. How come Mikalus hadn't ripped Carmichael a new one the moment he was resurrected?

"Apparently, and this is absolutely top secret and I don't think anyone else knows, it was Carmichael who killed Mikalus. For years, Cerberus had been doing what they did, but they were different times a few hundred years ago, obviously. Mikalus and Cerberus were not the best of friends, as Mikalus loved, still loves, his books. The book you got, the one that Aurelius wanted, it belonged to Mikalus, one of his library. Carmichael infiltrated his home, probably using the Teleron is the best guess, and he stole the book. Apparently he opened it, removed the protection around it, and Aurelius appeared. Shit got serious, things got smashed, windows and the like, and the sun streamed in. That was the end of Mikalus."

"Wow. That's... that's intense."

"What's in the book?" asked Vicky.

"Oh, this is the real shocker." Shocker? In the excitement Ivan had started to talk differently, losing his clipped mannerisms and controlled, slow way of speech, now babbling like Vicky. "This was how vampires were made." Ivan eyed us expectantly but all we did was stare at him blankly.

"Huh?" I managed.

"The book. Everyone thinks Mikalus summoned a demon and it turned him vampire. That's not true. Vampires, the First, Mikalus, got turned when he deciphered part of the book. Just a page. He discovered its secrets, read it, and something came. Not a demon, but an angel. It bit him."

"What the fuck? An angel turned him into a vampire?"

"Yes. The book holds countless such secrets, things we can't even dream of. It's basically a book of directions and also summoning spells, chants, whatever you call them, to allow you to become, well, I don't really know. But there are pages and pages of them. If you understand the book, then things will happen to you. You could change, become things we have never even dreamed of."

"This is nuts. And Aurelius, what does he have to do with it?"

"He was the one sent to retrieve it, but it's not that easy. He tried when Carmichael got it, when it was unprotected, and Mikalus ended up dead."

"But who wrote the damn thing?"

"I have no idea. I don't even think Mikalus does. If he does he didn't tell me. But there you have it. Mikalus was turned by an angel because it had no choice. My guess is the book holds a way to make angels do your bidding, do things they know how to do but won't unless you make them. He learned about vampires, decided he wanted to be one, then made the angel do it."

"Fuck. Um, and Carmichael, what's he?"

"Why, isn't it obvious?"

"Um, no."

"He's a vampire."

"Fuck."

"So you said," chortled Ivan, looking extremely smug. "Carmichael knew what Mikalus had done. Cerberus finds these things out. They probably got the information from a member of Mikalus' staff or something, and that's what all this is about. He broke in, and he got himself turned so he could continue to fight Mikalus. It ended badly, for Mikalus anyway, and ever since then the book was missing."

"Until you found it."

"Exactly. It was safe where it was, and Mikalus should have left it there. Sitting in a library, nobody knowing what it was, no threat, but as soon as you took it, the angels remembered about it, and it was back on their radar."

"You mean they forgot about it?"

"Apparently. Seems being an immortal angel messes with your memory." Ivan shrugged. "I assume Carmichael didn't keep hold of the book when he got Mikalus killed and some enterprising vampire hid it away, sure it was important."

"Great, so what you're telling us is Cerberus is headed by a dude who will willingly become vampire just so he can fight vampires and continue to ensure nobody else ever learns how to do it or use magical items. That's serious dedication."

"I know. Scary, right?"

"You aren't exactly making me keen to do this job."

"You promised. And besides, it's best to have all the information you can."

Ivan stood, leaving us shell-shocked, and said, "Farewell, I have to rest now. And don't forget, either of you. This is private, never to be told."

We nodded numbly, overwhelmed by the revelations.

At the doors, Ivan turned and said, "Do it soon."

"Yeah, we will. Give us some time to prepare though. This is, well, it's kind of impossible."

"I know."

"Oh, there's something in your car you need to dispose of," I said, suddenly remembering. "You should be more careful, Ivan. It was a Hound, I recognized him. Maybe up the vetting process for Vicky's staff?"

Ivan nodded, said nothing, then left.

"Why did you agree to the job? I thought you'd say no," asked Vicky, genuinely surprised and now looking about as keen as I felt to go through with this.

"Because, my dear munchkin, I am honor bound. And without honor I am nothing but a wrinkled old man with a stick in his pocket."

"At least it isn't flaccid," said Vicky with a smile and a nod at the Hat's nether regions.

"Amen to that."

Going Home

Vicky and I chatted for the next half hour but we hardly even got started on what was to be the biggest job of both our careers before the terrible twosome made an appearance and began doing what young girls seemed to do best. Namely, running around like they were mainlining sugar, coming and going only to return in different fancy dress costumes, and insisting that we admire their princess outfits, their tutus, and myriad characters I failed to guess at because I didn't watch kid's TV.

Grown-up time was definitely over.

Vicky and I would talk again tomorrow. Maybe. I went to leave then cursed as I realized Ivan had left me without a way to get back to the city. Where was my bloody car? I called Ivan and after an annoying wait was told his goon had dropped it in the city center, the muppet. So I called a taxi and got taken for a ride, both literally and monetarily. Goddamn, no wonder people used apps to call for services where anybody with a vehicle could act as a taxi.

When I got to my car, I realized I hadn't asked Ivan where his new place was, so messaged him and got given the address. It sounded just about right. Still grungy enough to satisfy the guys on the street, but comfortable for him too. He'd hated his swanky apartment so had finally found something more suitable. Not that I planned on visiting him, but it was best to have the information just in case.

And so it was, by mid-morning, that I found myself at somewhat of a loose end. I'd been up all night, unable to sleep so I'd prowled the city streets, had a workout, something to eat, other stuff you don't need to know about, so I was running on fumes now. Somehow, I made it back to my semi in the city, went through my portal, got in another car once I exited the gate at the barn, drove home to the farm, and only felt the weight of the world shucked off my shoulders when I took off my boots, walked through my house, and entered the delight that was my kitchen.

Ah, my beautiful kitchen. Clean, tidy, sparkling, and mine. I'd upgraded several items these last few months, so the cooker still had clean grills, the oven shone as once they get dirty even the most obsessive of wizards can't get them clean, even with magic, and I'd bought one of those crazy expensive taps that give instant boiling water and has a hose to help clean up. I'd also upgraded the coffee machine until I had my own mini cafe, a model Candy had approved of and helped me pick.

Going shopping with a woman had felt impossibly strange, something I hadn't done for the longest time, although George had dragged me around clothes stores once and I nearly had a seizure. But this was different, proper shopping with a purpose. We'd laughed and joked, had fun, and for once I'd actually felt like a normal human being.

I started the gleaming black and chrome machine and pottered about making myself coffee, enjoying the quiet and sense of familiar, then sat with a sweet Americano at my table and just soaked up the silence.

For the next hour I went over the conversation we'd had with Ivan, the revelations, the gaps in it all and the things left unsaid, probably unasked, and tried to figure out how it would impact my future, and Vicky's. It honestly didn't make a lot of difference. Carmichael was still the face of Cerberus, they still wanted all the artifacts, and he'd still be after my blood, vampire or not. It was valuable information nonetheless, but what was more valuable was the information about vampires themselves.

I'd known that their strength lay in how strong their maker was, but hadn't quite understood how it worked or the true significance and disparity between them all. Or how they fed. I'd assumed some were basically monsters, killers of the innocent, but Ivan, same as other vampires, insisted that wasn't the case and I was prone to believe him. They were people, sort of, and most people would balk at murder.

But a hundred thousand of them? That was a lot. I wondered why there was a limit, but decided some things just had to be accepted. So that's what I did.

Most importantly of all, and what concerned me above all else, was the job. How the hell was I going to achieve this? Could I? Yes, I could, because then I'd owe Ivan nothing, satisfy the vampires, and really piss off Carmichael and Cerberus.

And then there was Vicky. She was acting too content with her new place, and I could see it was a facade. She was wired, looking for trouble, and it was only a matter of time before she went off the rails again. If I could have kept her out of this I would have, but that wasn't an option as if I tried, she'd get herself into even more trouble.

So, all I had to do was keep Vicky contained, keep the vampires happy, not get myself killed, and go steal what couldn't be stolen. Shouldn't be a problem, not for The Hat.

I smiled at my own joke. This was impossible; I was screwed. Maybe I could leave the country, buy a hut on a remote island somewhere and live out my days eating coconuts and lazing in a hammock. Maybe I'd even sleep.

At the thought, I drained my coffee and hauled my sorry ass upstairs to try to get some shut-eye.

Panic Stations

I woke up with a start, head pounding, tongue feeling like somebody had knitted it a little sweater then slipped it on while I slept fitfully. I also needed to pee real bad.

Once relieved, at least in the bladder sense, I stumbled about my bedroom in my birthday suit and tried not to look at myself in the mirror. I failed miserably. Everyone's drawn to the scene of the crime, right?

Eventually, I gave up all pretense, and took a long hard look at myself. Candy and I had been doing all right, taking it slow, going out on dates, getting to know each other, even had a nice fumble, but that was as far as it had gone. I was surprised at myself, as my lust levels were high and so were her breasts, but I hadn't tried anything on and she hadn't had to slap me silly.

But, if things went well, there would come a time when I'd bring her up to my bedroom and we'd get naked. The thought of it was awesome, at least the her being naked part, but me, not so much. I'd been visiting Beast more often, watching what I ate, even tried taming the hair and beard, but the stubble kept growing, the hair seemed to live by a set of rules that had different ideas about gravity to the rest of me, and said gravity was being stubbornly insistent about dragging my flesh down low.

As I stared in the mirror for the first time in several months, I was pleasantly surprised by what I saw. I'd leaned out, although I was always lean, but in that way where you're skinny with loose skin. Now everything had finally tightened up. I was wiry, that's what I was. I looked strong, toned, even had abs, kind of.

Not bad at all for an insomniac wizard in his forties who liked his fry-up and kept very irregular hours. But Candy was much younger than me and had a figure to die for. Would this suffice? Yes, it would. I'd never been fat, always tried to exercise, and I knew I looked better than a lot of dudes half my age. All the running away from the bad guys will keep a wizard in trim.

I knew I was being hard on myself, overly critical, but I had standards and got severely pissed if I failed to live up to them. Same went for magic and everything else in my life. I expected too much so got disappointed when life didn't turn out how I wanted.

Time to put that behind me, be more positive. As I peered closely at my face, dragged down the skin beneath my eyes, smoothed over the wrinkles and tried to tame my hair, I smiled. This was me, nothing I could do about it. A man with a face that showed the varied life he'd had, the life he enjoyed. And that was the most important thing—I enjoyed my life. I had my daughter, a couple of friends, okay maybe two, a faery godmother who had been suspiciously absent of late, and I had a super-hot shifter who seemed to like me.

Awesome!

So I checked my watch to see when I should get ready, then almost had a heart attack when I saw the time. Hell, I'd been in bed all day. I'd tossed and turned for an age, the usual routine, but must have dropped off eventually and slept for hours.

Panicked, as I hated being late, and Candy wasn't the kind of woman to take kindly to being left waiting, I showered, argued with my hair again, and lost, again, dressed in clean combats, a new brown shirt, and rushed downstairs acting like a dizzy teenager.

"Hey, George," I panted in a panic as I patted my pockets frantically.

"Hey, Dad." George, most beautiful woman in the world, smiled sympathetically at me, her green eyes sparkling, her auburn hair shining like God himself had brushed it after he made her long curls out of fluffy clouds.

"Ugh, where is it?" I moaned, getting stressed as I tried to remember where all my pockets were—a wizard needs lots.

"It's where it always is. In your oh-so-secret pocket on the right side of your combats."

"Ugh, yeah, right. Thanks." I reached down to the same pocket I'd reached into a million times and felt the reassuring hardness of my wand. Hell, what was wrong with me?

"Big date, eh?"

"Yeah, and I'm late. I'm never late. Damn, I'm all over the place."

"You like her, huh?"

"I guess," I said, distracted as I pulled out a spoon from a pocket I didn't know I had. "Here, have this. Gotta go." I gave a grinning George the spoon, rushed off, then turned and ran back, kissed her sweetly perfumed head and said, "Love you, honey."

"Love you too, Dad."

As I hopped about like an electrocuted frog trying to get my boots on, I could hear George's laughter from the kitchen.

Then I was out the door, dodging chickens in the cobbled courtyard, and soon enough I was away, driving through country lanes so I could get to my barn, through the portal, make it to the city, and go meet Candy.

The life of a wildcat wizard is never easy, especially with so many pockets.

Date with Trouble

I was in such a panic by the time I'd got to the city and dashed around the streets looking for my car—I think I got the right one but could never be sure—that as I buckled up and drove off, I realized I had no idea where on earth I was going.

What were we doing this evening? Where were we meeting?

I drew an utter blank.

What should I do? Call Candy and ask her? No, bad idea, Arthur. You don't impress ladies by admitting you forgot where you were meeting, that does not lead to sexy times and sweaty bodies writhing in your bed. What it leads to is being hung up on and having to find somewhere else to get coffee.

Fighting the urge to slam my head into the steering wheel and bang my hands against said head, I fought down the rising panic and told myself that I would not lose the plot. I would remain calm and cool.

I failed miserably. Several minutes later, after I'd pulled over and ranted and raved and just beaten the shit out of the steering wheel as a safer compromise to using my head, I leaned back, sweating and gasping, and finally got a grip of myself.

Think, Arthur, think. Where were you meant to meet this beautiful woman?

Bar? No, don't like bars. Restaurant? Nope, that didn't ring a bell. Zoo? Idiot, it's the evening. What do people do in the evening? Cinema! Yes, that was it. The cinema.

Fuck! Where was the cinema?

I had absolutely no idea. I didn't go to the cinema, never had time. Plus, George had said the popcorn was really expensive.

Finally, feeling like an utter fool, I caved and phoned George. She laughed at me, but I got the info I needed and headed off to an out-of-town complex that housed the cinema, chain restaurants and such-like.

I parked up, ran across the packed car-park, my watch saying six thirty exactly, and skidded to a halt outside the entrance, smiling at my bravery and skills of deduction. Panting, I discreetly wiped myself down, as a sweaty date is not a pleasant thing.

Five minutes later, I was tapping my foot impatiently and wondering why she was late. I went into the foyer and checked for her but there was no sign. So I sidled up to the board showing the times and stared blankly. There was nothing new starting until eight. Why had we arranged to meet so early? A drink first maybe? I wasn't sure, this was her idea.

I checked my phone but there was no missed call, then I scrolled through my messages and read the one from Candy confirming our date, and the time.

"You fucking idiot," I whispered to myself, as there were kids around, chattering manically as they emerged from the movie theater.

Angry with myself, I wandered outside to get some air, and read the message again.

"See you at seven thirty, hot stuff."

Bollocks. I was an hour early. Then I read the bit about hot stuff again and smiled.

At least I wasn't late, that had to be worth a gold star, right?

A Pit Stop

The movie was crap, the company was awesome. I spent most of the grueling two hours fifteen minutes and twenty-seven seconds staring at Candy. She didn't seem to notice, was engrossed in the humongous screen.

Outside, with the sky dark, or as dark as you get in a crowded metropolis, the neon glaring from the "restaurants," Candy said, "Fancy a coffee at mine?"

My heart leapt and I gulped then said, "That sounds nice," and walked her to my car as fast as I could without seeming too eager. She'd got a taxi, which was a good sign, so things were looking up.

Candy gave me directions and I obeyed without thinking, my focus on what was to come.

"I saw you looking, you know?" she said, her eyes dancing with mirth when I glanced her way.

"Don't know what you mean?" I said, acting all casual as is my way.

"During the movie. You kept looking at me."

"Only because you're beautiful."

"Charmer," she said, then chuckled. "Take a right here, then first left, then another right."

I did as I was told, mind elsewhere, then she said, "Here we are. Don't know why you needed directions though." She looked at me funny, and as I pulled up and turned off the engine it was only then that my mind clicked into gear and I realized where I was.

"Your cafe? Um, yeah, great."

"Oh, haha, when I said fancy a coffee you thought I meant my place?"

"Um, yeah, kinda."

"We can go if you want? I, er, sorry, I didn't think. Was just making a night of it, thought it would be fun. I've never been here late, never opened up just for a guy I like."

"Honestly, don't sweat it. It's a great idea, very nice. Come on, let's go drink coffee by candlelight and I can stare into your eyes and you can count my wrinkles."

"Okay, old man, let's do it."

We held hands, crossed the quiet road, and headed for Candy's tiny coffee shop wedged between two tall buildings like a squashed box.

I hadn't had this much fun in ages. Not since our last date. I didn't once think of what Ivan wanted me to do. About Vicky or George or anything but my own happiness, so, as I thought that I felt guilty. Damn, it was all right to have fun, wasn't it? I hadn't done stuff like this for so long it was hard to know how to do it.

Candy squeezed my hand as we walked and asked, "You okay?"

"Great, absolutely great." I returned the squeeze and felt her warm fingers tight against mine.

Nice.

Candy slid her hand free, our fingers playing their own games, the tips electric as they touched for a moment before we released, and she smiled at me as she unlocked the door. Goddamn, she was so awesome. Inside, she moved expertly to the back and switched on the machine in the dark then came back with two red candles that she placed on the counter. The red light made her look even more alluring, highlighting her cheekbones, dark shadows where her body curved.

We stared at each other, the tension rising, dare I say smoldering, saying nothing until the hiss of the machine broke us from our dreams of naughtiness. Candy busied herself making coffee and I could tell by her haste that things were hotting up. Me, I was on fire. The last thing I needed was coffee.

She placed two espressos down on the counter and winked. "Thought something quick to drink would be a good idea. Hey," she said, as if the idea had just come to her, "I haven't seen your house yet."

"That's right," I said, smiling, "you haven't, have you? Wanna see?"

"Ooh, yes please."

I was burning up. The candlelight, her sparkling eyes, her golden hair, her smell, the aroma of coffee, and the caffeine that hit as I downed my drink in a few sips, it was all getting too much.

The bell above the door rang and spoiled it all.

Bugger.

Who Me?

"Kill the old fucker first," said a very handsome man a moment after he flicked on the lights. "And hurry up, I've got things to do." He stared at us, then seemingly as an afterthought, said, "Oh, hey, Candy."

He ran a hand through typical hipster style hair, rubbed his shiny beard, and stepped confidently into the cafe. Two similarly styled guys with the usual smart but casual gear and hair, plus the beards waxed to within an inch of their hairy lives, fanned out best they could in the poky room and advanced on me, grinning like the twats they were. Dead twats soon enough.

"You ruined my date," I growled. I turned to Candy and she was stiff as a rod, clenching her teeth and looking like she was trying not to appear scared. "Friends of yours?"

"No. Best you leave, Arthur. This isn't your fight."

"Arthur here isn't going anywhere. Like I said, he's going to die, then you. Teach you both a lesson."

"I'm good," I said. "I don't need any lessons, and trust me, there's nothing you can teach me. What's this all about?"

"None of your business," the guy snapped as all three reached us.

"You just made it my business. We were having a nice time, you spoiled it. We had candles."

"Sorry, but the date's over, grandpa."

Grandpa? The cheeky git.

I leaned over the counter, slowly blew out the candles, then asked Candy, "You okay? You want me to kill them?"

"No, this isn't your problem. It's mine. I'll deal with it."

"You sure?"

"Oh," she said, licking her lips, "absolutely." With that, Candy dropped down behind the counter so the guys couldn't see, but I was still leaning right over so I got an excellent view as she ripped off her blouse, yanked off her shoes and jeans, then dropped to all fours, all within a second. Oh boy, she was incredible on a level I hadn't even dreamed of.

Her body cracked and groaned and bits blunted as others sharpened. Hair changed, grew all along her back and then her entire body, and her underwear slipped off her as she shrank to the size of a very nice looking Border Collie. Shame she hadn't taken the underwear off first, but you can't have everything you want.

I turned and said, "Look, guys, I don't know what this is about, but can't we—" I was rudely interrupted by a punch to the face, which I saw coming but let happen for one simple reason. While the leader of this small group of misfits was hitting me he wasn't doing much of anything else, so as his fist was busy connecting with my face, I was busy pulling out my wand.

My head snapped back with the punch but I stayed exactly where I was, which took the guy by surprise.

"You finished?" I asked.

"Just getting started, mate." He stared at me for a moment then asked, "Who are you?" and I saw a flicker of if not recognition then a recalling of a story or two about me.

"I'm the fucking Hat, asswipe." I grinned, licked the blood trickling from my nose, and said, "Look down."

His eyes lowered to where my wand was sticking into his belly, the shock registering. He knew what it was. Which meant he was from the supernatural world, and my guess was, as this was the style most assumed at this time, he was one of the Wild Ones. Shifters.

"Candy?" I didn't want to kill him without her say-so, and she'd said she'd deal with it, plus I was still clinging to the hope of sexy times later on.

Right on cue, a set of paws appeared on the counter and the rest of her soon after. For a moment, Candy stood immobile, a lovely collie but with canines bared. She growled and snapped at the air; my attention was diverted.

The dude took several steps back, away from my wand, and his guys followed suit.

Before I knew what was happening, they were all mostly naked and shifting into one animal or another. We had a mangy looking dog, a fox, and the main guy became a large Labrador.

Shit was about to get real.

Wowzer

I'd heard all about Candy's reputation. She was, sorta, kinda, a bit like the leader of a group of Wild Ones. They worked together, they played together, and they fought others. Some, make that most, shifters were unstable, violent, and unable to control themselves in the slightest once in animal form. They lost themselves to the creature within and it was only once the fight was over and the threat eliminated that they came back to themselves.

Candy's group was a little different in that they were smart, helped each other out, and were the go-to people for those in the know who wanted a certain kind of protection, or jobs done that fell somewhere between "utterly illegal" and "could get you killed."

Guess I like my women with similar interests to my own. Plus, she was hot and ran a nice cafe.

So I shouldn't have been surprised at the level of violence she showed, but I was. I was taken aback by the ferocity of her and the others as they fought as true animals. Wild, with utter abandon, fearless, and unwilling to back down. It put my shenanigans to shame.

Candy may not have been the largest, but she was the best fighter by a long shot.

She sprang from the counter, using my shoulders to leap directly into battle. I was pushed back hard against the counter as she launched, and it was there I remained.

My sweet date landed on the back of the fox, not much smaller than her, and simply bit down hard on the back of its neck. She tore away flesh and fur with a ragged whipping of the head that made me wince. The fox yowled like it had been caught by a pack of hunting hounds and then its feet splayed out. It died moments later as Candy tugged a mouthful of flesh from its neck and spat it away like it was poison.

Without pause, Candy leaped straight at the much larger Labrador and went right for the throat. The lab was fast and whipped its head around just in time. Their jaws snapped and shook as they grabbed each other's muzzles in a ferocious display I knew from experience could lead to serious injury, even death. But they untangled their teeth from each other and Candy whipped around as the lab retreated to gather itself. She tore into the other dog, a thick-furred mongrel, before it knew what was coming.

Candy was all animal, little human left inside as she fought. It was without malice or compassion or anything but the primitive drive to survive. She nipped at the belly of the dog as it whimpered and skidded on the tiles and slipped onto its side. The cries of a dog in distress are disturbing like no other noise I have ever heard. There's something about it that gets right to your most basic emotions, and part of me wanted to rush forward and save the poor creature. But this wasn't my fight, Candy wanted to deal with this the way the Wild Ones did. They all knew what they were getting themselves involved in.

With a final vicious shake of her head, she split the soft flesh covering the abdomen of the fallen dog and then, as guts spilled out, she clamped down tight on its throat and shook in a death grip that nothing could make her release. The dying dog's eyes turned up in its head until only the whites could be seen and then it was over. She released and yowled as the Labrador sank its teeth deep into her rear, spinning in pain and shock, shucking off the creature as she did so.

This was all so fast, so utterly manic, that it was hard to follow the action, but I was entranced, mesmerized by this most violent and base of displays. Was this how I looked when I fought? Did I lose all control and act on instinct alone? I guess I did.

Being in the middle of a fight is a beautiful thing in its own way. You are consumed by the moment, think nothing of friends and family, of the wider world, are focused like a laser on your next move and that of your opponent, on survival. Everything is compressed until all that exists is the movement of your own body and that of your foe, the adrenaline surging then peaking as you rain down bloody hell on them and try to stop them doing the same in return.

You are alive like at no other time, and watching this display, I understood that this was about as pure a way of living as there was. Everything else was shoved aside, leaving you bare, exposed, your true self, your base nature revealed.

Only problem being, it hurts like hell when you get hit, bitten, or blasted with magic, so there's always a downside. But even the pain is subdued when you're really going for it, the signals from the nerves dampened so they don't interfere with your reactions, and it is only afterward that you emerge into a world of hurt you hadn't believed possible.

But if you win? Oh, the glory, the sense of satisfaction, the high you get.

At least, that's what it used to be like. At this time I was past most of that, didn't get much of anything apart from a deep sadness that there was still so much violence in the world and I was part of the problem not the solution. But there was always that glimmer, that heightening of the senses, and, yes, a glow of satisfaction. Of fighting yet another bad guy and emerging triumphant.

Candy was obviously feeling all of this in full. She was panting, and I swear she was smiling, adrenaline coursing, hackles raised, eyes focused on the large dog snarling as it charged.

She had very good senses, and excellent reactions, and as the lab sprang at her, dwarfing her, she crouched. As the dog sailed overhead, she snapped out fast at its belly. Not well enough to spill blood, but it sent her attacker tumbling across the floor.

She was on it in a second.

Candy jumped onto the dog's belly and snapped at its face, but it shook its head manically, making it hard for her to latch on. Frustrated, and snarling in anger, Candy clamped down on an ear, biting half of it off to the screams of her fallen opponent. There was a mad scramble as they both shook this way and that, and then they were back on their feet, squaring off against each other.

They leaped simultaneously, hit mid-air, and crashed down in a tangle of legs.

Things got intense then, the dogs locked together and moving so fast it was impossible to see what was happening.

Finally, Candy walked carefully back, cautious and eyes locked on this most unwelcome of guests. The dog was still, blood covered its fur in matted clumps, but she was taking no chances. For several long seconds she watched. Then she moved forward slowly, and just before she reached the Labrador it shook violently and attacked.

It was exhausted, though, almost gone, and the fight was already over. Candy sidestepped easily and swatted it like an oversized fly, sending it skidding into the wall where it crunched in a heap. She ran forward and locked her muzzle on its neck, holding her position as the dog shook then was still.

Then, and only then, did she release her grip and move away, head held high, tail wagging sluggishly, body quivering with the outpouring of energy and violence.

And then she changed. Her fur receded, her limbs grew, her head shook in a blur until her beautiful features returned, and then her naked body was before me, covered in patches of blood, lithe and strong and pumped up from the exertion. A naked Candy on all fours, hot and sweaty and sticky and breathing deep.

I gaped, I gulped, and then I said, "You got a bite on your bum."

Candy wiggled it experimentally, maybe thinking she still had a tail, maybe not, and I gripped the counter tightly so I didn't fall over.

Trust me, I've had worse dates. Much worse.

A Warm Bed

Candy sprang to her feet, the animal inside receding but not gone. She whipped her head around to stare at me and I held my hands up and said, "Whoa, it's me, remember?"

For a moment she just wasn't there, human but still inhuman, an inner battle waging between one and the other. But then she shook, her mess of hair tussled and wild. And super sexy. It felt wrong to be so entranced by her in this state, after what she'd done, but I was only human and I couldn't help it. Was it the violence that excited me, or was it the sight of her so sweaty and bouncy and naked? Probably all of it, if I'm honest.

She advanced, slowly, and I would have taken a step back if I wasn't already against the counter. She got close, so close I could smell her musk, and then she said, "I remember," and winked at me.

Candy leaped the counter in a move as graceful as a gymnast, and I kept my eyes diverted as that would have just been rude. Instead, I watched as the dead

Wild Ones shifted back into human form, which was not a pretty sight. Candy reappeared then, clothes back on, looking amped up and breathing heavily.

"Did you stare at my bum?" she asked, deathly serious.

Damn, I guess I broke most of the rules of decorum and decency staring at her like that. Probably not the done thing when shifters change back and forth, but c'mon!

"Um, maybe, a little. You were bitten, it was just to inspect the wound.

"So, you're a doctor then?"

"Not a medical one, no."

"Oh," she asked, hands on hips, "what kind of doctor are you then?"

"Obvious, isn't it?" I said, grinning despite myself. "I'm a doctor of love."

Candy gave me the evil eye, but her smile spread, and then she was laughing. She'd been messing with me. Damn! "Arthur, that is, beyond doubt, the worst line I have ever heard."

"I've got others," I offered.

"It does hurt a little," she said, patting her posterior.

"I can take a better look if you like? I've got a mini pharmacy at my place. Could patch you right up." I was pushing it, but a guy had to give it his best shot.

"Who could refuse such an offer? Let's go."

"Um, what about these guys? And who the hell were they?"

"I'll make a call. And I'll tell you all about it. Later."

The later was a tantalizing prospect. Did she mean, later, like on the way to my house? Or did she mean later, like in the morning?"

While I pondered such important mysteries, Candy made a call. Then we left.

I had a problem now. Candy, like most other folk in this dangerous world I made my way through, didn't know about my gates, didn't know where I lived or much about my private life. She knew I had a daughter, knew I lived on a farm, but not where. Should I tell her, or just take her to the city house?

I decided, and it was no easy decision, because I'd vowed never to let George meet any of the few women in my life unless I was fairly certain things would lead somewhere. I didn't want her disappointed, growing attached to somebody only for them to be gone. Candy was lovely though, and had been great company, and so I decided to take her home.

We made it to the semi and entered, Candy quiet, me the same. There was tension, thick and insistent, but I didn't want to stay here. This wasn't my home, it was a halfway house between one world and the other. My world.

"Okay, here's the deal. This is private, never to be told to another person."

"Agreed."

"Good. I don't live here, it's just somewhere to pop in for a cuppa and to house my gates."

"Er, what, you collect gates?" asked Candy, nonplussed and probably wondering how to call this off.

"No, not collect. I own two gates, they're portals. They take you from one place to another. The one here leads to my real home. Do you want to come to my real home?"

"Of course. But gates? You mean like magical portals?" she asked, laughing.

"Yes, that's exactly what I mean."

"Oh."

"So, hold on to my hand and do not, and I cannot stress this enough, let go. It'll hurt," I warned.

"Can't wait," she said, but I could tell she didn't believe, not really. You wouldn't, would you?

Several minutes later, she believed all right, and as she gasped and oohed and aahed and things heated up, as a fight and a trip through a magic doorway can really get the juices flowing, we were driving to my farm.

The house was quiet, George was asleep, but we were wired. I showed Candy my kitchen and she approved, ran her hands along the counter, admired the new tap, even commented on my cutlery drawer, which was nice.

"I have an en-suite, the medical kit's up there," I said, pushing my luck but hoping this was where it was all heading. Had I really held off for nine months? I had. Maybe I'd taken it a little too slow? But it felt right, that this should not be rushed. Now, those months of abstinence were ready to burst free.

"Then fix me up good, Doc."

Clothes were off within seconds of me closing the door to my bedroom, and it wasn't until many hours later that we finally got around to patching up her injuries. After the acrobatics, I was pretty sure I'd need a doctor to realign my spine and sort out the muscle spasms, as Candy was energetic and I was definitely out of practice.

But the best thing of all? What made this probably the best night of my entire life? I slept, oh boy did I sleep. I slept with my arm wrapped around her gently curved belly, feeling her warmth snuggled into me, the smell of her in my throat, filling my senses and my dreams, warm and comforting and wanting to be here beside me.

I slept like a baby and I never wanted it to end.

And when I opened my eyes, with birds chirping, their happy song lifting my spirits even higher, and with the sun shining and the bed warm, the pillow smelling of her perfume, she was gone.

Crowded Kitchen

My heart sank for a moment, but then I put my sensible hat on—my other one was somewhere in the room along with my clothes—and decided not to just freak out. She'd have left to open up the coffee shop, right?

Duh, not likely. We were a long way from the city, she had no car, and she definitely didn't know how to use the portal. Then I panicked about that. What if she'd tried to go through the gate and now she was just dust floating around the Nolands, never to be seen again?

Deciding I would find out soon enough, and finding it impossible to feel too glum because, you know, sex with a hot woman, lots of sex, I stretched out my limbs, muscles aching more than after a session with Beast, hurting in places I didn't know were places, then, after my body had cricked and creaked and I did some groaning, I showered, fought my hair in a battle I'd never won, and got dressed.

The sound of laughter greeted me from the kitchen as I approached, and that made me wary. I crept in cautiously, worrying about spillages and misuse of spatulas—the silicone green one was for eggs only, I don't know how many times I had to repeat such a simple concept—then stopped dead in my tracks, saw what was about to greet me, and stepped back into the hall as silently as a mouse.

"Hey, Dad," said George, staring right at me from her place at the table facing the hall.

"Um, hey," I mumbled, wondering if fathers were allowed to run away and leave girlfriends in the kitchen.

"Morning, handsome," said Candy. She turned and winked at me, which brought girlish tittering from George and Vicky. Yeah, that's right, Vicky was there too. Hell, all it needed was for Sasha, faery godmother extraordinaire, to turn up and the ensemble would be complete.

"You look tired," said Vicky, which brought more tittering from the women. I think I might have blushed.

"Busy night," I said, foolishly stepping forward into my, yes, my, kitchen.

"I bet," said Vicky.

"Um, morning," I said to Candy as I approached, and for the life of me I don't know what possessed me, what I was thinking, and it was just automatic anyway, but I put my hand out and ruffled the top of her head, getting my fingers tangled in her hair.

The room went silent, Candy stared at me like I'd lost the plot, Vicky sighed, and George just shook her head in disappointment.

"I told you," said George. "He's utterly clueless."

"He's an idiot," agreed Vicky.

"I think it's cute. He's gone all shy, feels uncomfortable. Don't you, sweetie?" asked Candy as she stood up and, without inhibition, kissed me. Yum.

"Sorry, this is, er, all new to me. I didn't mean anything by it, just, er, hell, will you all stop staring at me. Why is everyone so relaxed? Shouldn't I introduce everyone, and, er, is this okay, George?"

"Dad, it's fine. I'm a big girl now and besides, I've had boys..."

"Boys, what?" I asked, maybe growled. "I hope you weren't about to say you'd had boys over, as I certainly haven't seen any and you're too young and no daughter of mine is going to—"

"Arthur, calm down, you're going to blow a gasket," said Candy.

George grinned, Vicky shook her head in increasing despair, and me, I slumped into a chair, beaten, and when the air took on a familiar tingle and faery dust fell onto the table, I just groaned and put my head in my hands.

"Good morning," said Sasha brightly, looking like a million dollars and scaring the hell out of Candy.

"Morning," we all chorused, but Candy just stared.

"Did you... Did she... Are you really?"

"She did. She is," I said glumly.

"Wow!" said Candy. They'd met several times, and she knew the story a little, not a lot, a little, but it's one thing being told something, another seeing it happen.

"Ah, so Arthur finally got his act together and got into your pants, did he?" asked Sasha as faery dust fell down her cleavage and I looked away.

"If you don't mind, can we keep this respectable?" I said. "My daughter is here and I won't have you talk like that to my girlfriend," I said. In response, everyone stared at me again.

"Girlfriend?" asked Candy, raising a perfect eyebrow.

Oh, damn, had I blown it? We hadn't had this conversation. Hadn't talked about whether we were exclusive. I'd just assumed we were, as I was old-fashioned and wouldn't dream of dating more than one woman at a time, but knew the younger generation went in for that kind of thing.

"Um, well, if you want to be?" I asked, feeling like a damn fool.

"He's so sweet when he's squirming," said Sasha, who, along with all the other women in the room, of which there were three too many, leaned forward to better make me feel like an utter dick.

"Sounds nice. I'll cancel my dates with the others for the rest of the week," said Candy.

"Oh."

"I'm joking, I only date one handsome wizard at a time."

That perked me right up, and I stuck my tongue out at the others. Everyone laughed and that was that, one big happy family.

We had breakfast, all of us, drank coffee, avoided talking about what had gone on between me and Candy the previous evening, and every so often I'd catch George's eye and ask if she was okay, wanting to ensure she didn't mind a woman coming downstairs that she didn't know. Especially with it being obvious she'd slept with her father.

I'd underestimated her, and she was cool about it. Didn't seem phased in the slightest.

After torturing me by insisting on doing the washing up, Vicky took Candy off to show her around and I had a few minutes alone with George. Sasha had already gone, only staying long enough to watch the Arthur Feeling Like a Right Twat Show.

"Are you okay with this?" I asked. "I didn't want to bring anyone home unless I was pretty sure about them. Um, not that I've had the chance until now anyway. But I don't want you to feel uncomfortable, and if you don't want me to then I won't."

"Dad, it's fine. Look, I know you're a man, okay? I know you're looking out for me, and I appreciate it. It's so nice you're thinking about me, but it's your house, your life. You do what you want."

"Yes, but I don't want you getting attached to anyone just in case... Anyway, it's your house too. We're partners. A family."

"Look, I'm not pining for a mother figure. If you want a girlfriend I think that's awesome. You deserve it.

Plus, er, we've met a few times before." George twiddled a lock of red hair as her eyes darted away.

"Who have you met before?" I asked, nonplussed.

"Candy. Once you said you were dating her, I, well, I went to the coffee shop and introduced myself. We've had a few chats, got to know each other."

"What! You should have said. Candy didn't say."

"That's because I asked her not to. I didn't want it to get weird, and I didn't know how it would go with you guys. I was, um, I was looking out for you. I wanted to check her out to make sure she was good enough."

"And is she?"

"Yeah, she seems really nice. Confident, takes no crap, but friendly and open. Plus, I bet she keeps you in line, right?"

I thought back to the trouble at the cafe and said, "You have no idea."

"And I know she's a shifter."

"She told you?" I was surprised.

"No, Vicky did."

"Damn big mouth."

We hugged then, and I said, "I love you. Thank you for being such a perfect daughter."

"Idiot," said George, but she hugged her old dad and my morning was as perfect as it could be.

Then Vicky came back in, and it went downhill rapidly.

Saying Goodbye

"You've forgotten, haven't you?" asked Vicky, hands on hips, staring in accusation.

"No, I haven't," I said, staring her down, trying not to get distracted by Candy as she moved around the kitchen like she was entirely at home.

"Okay then, what haven't you forgotten?" Vicky scrunched up her nose, then her eyes widened in shock as she glanced at Candy. "Um, don't answer that," she spluttered hurriedly.

"Fine, I won't," I said, without a single clue what on earth she was on about. "What are you doing here, anyway?"

Vicky huffed in exasperation and turned to George for moral support. "How do you put up with him"?

"You get used to it. He's distracted." George nodded in Candy's direction, who was inspecting my tap closely and making agreeable noises. Girl after my own heart. Nothing like seeing a woman admire a quality tap to know she's the one for you.

"Dad? Dad? Hello?"

"Eh, what?"

"I said you get distracted by... never mind."

"Oh, right. Okay then." I stood there like a lemon for a while, as this was all very new territory for me and I wasn't sure what the protocol was. What did I have to do today? Why was Vicky here?

As I stared around the room blankly, at a total loss, I must have zoned out, as the next thing I knew, Candy was tugging at my shirt sleeve and saying, "Is that okay?"

"Fine," I mumbled. "Um, what was the question again?"

Candy stood on tiptoe and peered into my eyes. "Arthur Salzman, if I talk to you will you do me the courtesy of listening?"

Wow, feisty!

George laughed, Vicky sniggered, and Candy kept glaring at me. People didn't talk to me like this. Okay, they did, but only the grinning fools at the table. Guess I had one more strong-willed woman to add to the list of ladies I adored that could handle The Hat.

I held my hands up and said, "I apologize. Okay, listen up everyone, as you're all watching me like I'm a freak show. This is all very strange, and I feel uncomfortable about the whole thing. I'm nervous because I don't want George getting upset with me bringing anyone home. I'm also not sure where this is going or how Candy feels, and I'm sure she could do without the intensity, and I know I'm not helping, so can we all please just act normal?" My voice was rising and I was waving my arms about, but that was it, all I had to say.

"Dad, I'm fine. I told you."

"I know, but I worry."

"Sorry," said Vicky.

"Arthur, honestly, everything is okay," said Candy, eyes softening as she put her hand on my shoulder. "We all know each other. I like George and Vicky, I like you, and to be honest, weird as it sounds, I feel at ease here, like I've been here loads of times."

"You sure?"

"Yeah, the only one making this odd is you, Dad," said George.

"Oh, right. Er, well, glad that's sorted then."

"Now, as I was saying before you began shouting and being weirder than usual, will you please take me back to the city? I have to get to work."

"Oh, damn, the cafe. Your customers will be annoyed."

"Don't worry, Teresa opened up. I asked her yesterday."

"Did you now?" I asked, smiling. Guess Candy had planned on making the night special.

"I did." Candy kissed me, and I didn't feel like a fool, or glance around to see who was looking. It was just nice, natural.

We left a few minutes later. The Hat had successfully navigated some rough terrain dealing with so many women in his kitchen and deserved a big pat on the back. I did pretty good, right?

We went through the portal without incident. Then we walked a few streets, found the car eventually, and I drove Candy to work. She had clothes and stuff there so no need to go home, although I still didn't know where home was.

Outside the door to the busy cafe, the smell of bitter coffee strong in the air, the windows steamed up, the heat of the day making the air thick with a haze I felt in my head and body, I uttered words difficult to say. "Can we go out again tomorrow? I have the feeling I'm busy tonight."

"That would be lovely. And Arthur?"

"Yeah?"

"Relax a little, okay? I know it's hard bringing someone home when you have a daughter, but George is a smart, resourceful girl. She made it her business to come see me and get to know me. She's a great girl. So relax, all right?"

"I'll try, but it isn't easy."

"Not the kind of bloke to chill out and not stress, are you?"

"You don't know the half of it," I muttered, wishing with all my heart that I could just relax. But, strangely, I did feel calm, lighter, and that was all down to this wonderful woman beside me.

"See you tomorrow. I had a lovely time. And trust me, you were great."

"Great?"

"You are so dense sometimes. The sex, Arthur. It was fantastic."

Saying nothing, as I was feeling too smug, I cupped her head gently between my rough hands and kissed her.

It was with a broad grin that I went on my merry way. Yeah, I know, but sometimes it's nice to hear confirmed what you try to convince yourself of. That being, The Hat still had it.

Getting It Together

The grin remained as I wandered the city streets in a smog of smugness. It wasn't just the compliment that had lifted my spirits, it was the whole thing. Not only had it been an awesome night with Candy, and I was commended for it, but everything had gone better than I could have imagined in the morning. And on top of all that I'd slept like a baby.

My body felt truly alive. Hardly anything ached, my head was clear, my thoughts sharp, and my senses alert in a way I'd forgotten they could be. I could hear better, smell better, taste better, and the lingering scent of her perfume filled my nostrils. Although that was probably wishful thinking, as the warm air and lack of even the slightest breeze meant the city was already thick with car fumes and the heat of too many bodies in too small a space.

I had to get away from here. I wasn't in the right frame of mind to wallow in this filth. I needed space and clean country air to enhance my mood, to keep my spirits high, and so I rushed through the streets, closed the door thankfully on my car, and was enveloped in silence as I hightailed it back to the countryside as fast as possible.

I think it was only about halfway home I even remembered the slaughter that had occurred in Candy's cafe the night before. No wonder the night had been impassioned. Violence can do funny things to you, and I guess both of us had been pretty hyped after such a display.

What that said about me, and her, I didn't want to dwell on, as it wouldn't lead to a good place.

And then I thought of Vicky. Damn, had I really forgotten what we'd agreed to do? I had. The most epic, mad, definitely impossible job ever and I'd forgotten all about it as I was overcome with lust and nerves about taking a nice lady home with me. I needed to get a grip, there was dangerous work to be done and I at least congratulated myself on not having made a date for this evening.

"Better get this over with," I grumbled as I stepped through the portal and into my barn.

I stood outside for a while, staring off to the distant sea, letting the breeze coming in ruffle my hair and smooth away my frown while I thought about what had to be done, and how I could pull it off.

I had absolutely no idea.

Vicky's Plan

"I've got it all worked out," said Vicky as she glanced up from her laptop then clacked away like a mad monkey with some Shakespeare to write. Her fingers were a blur as she hammered the poor device like it had been very naughty, and she kept running her tongue over her top teeth as she was prone to do when concentrating.

With a flourish, she assaulted several more keys, snapped the lid closed, leaned back, and folded her arms, looking impossibly pleased with herself.

"Good, because I haven't," I moaned, slumping into a chair at the table as my mood dropped and reality came crashing back in. "This is why you're here then? To go over what we're going to do?"

"Of course. So stop thinking of boobs and start thinking of the job."

"I was not thinking about boobs." I was.

"Liar. But I'm happy for you, Arthur, I really am. I like Candy, and admit it, she is way out of your league."

"But..." I spluttered, "you're the one who told me to ask her out. You said she liked me, that I was a catch. You said I was what women liked, that she'd say yes."

"Did I?" asked Vicky innocently. "Oh, well, I thought maybe there might be a chance, but she is younger than you, and very hot."

I went cold, then began to sweat. "Buster's hat, you mean I could have made a fool of myself? I thought you were sure she fancied me?"

"I was. Sort of. A bit."

"Ugh." I felt sick, but I guess it had worked out, so I should be grateful. And she was hot, and younger than me, although most women were. Single ones, anyway.

"Now, about my plan," said Vicky, with that mischievous glint in her eye I knew meant only one thing.

Trouble.

No Plan

"Absolutely not," I said after Vicky had spent half an hour laying out a "perfect plan" she could have explained in about three minutes.

"It's perfect," she protested.

"It is not. I am the expert, the mastermind, the one who devises the foolproof plan that always sees me get away with the goodies and have to drag you away before you ruin it."

"I do not."

"What about the time you 'accidentally' followed me inside and set off deadly gas in a strong room?"

"That was a one-off."

"Or the time you missed the electronic spears in that spooky house, and they started shooting out of the walls after I took the Brooch of Invisibility?"

"That wasn't my fault! And anyway, we had the brooch so we got away."

"Yeah, but the dog still ate my boots. Or the time that you said the alarm system was disabled and then I got locked in a cage and three monkeys, monkeys, actual monkeys, came screaming at me and I had to—"

"Yeah, yeah, so there have been a few minor mishaps, but this plan is amazing."

Calmly, not reveling in pointing out the many flaws in her plan, I went through her ideas and told her why it wouldn't work. I didn't count them off on my fingers and make fun of her lack of dastardly planning, or smile smugly, but I may have been grinning a little as I shot down her ideas.

"Spoilsport," said Vicky, sulking after I'd finished.

"If it's any consolation, your plan is still better than mine."

"Why, what's yours?"

"I haven't got one."

"Oh."

"Yet."

My Plan

For the next several hours, while George popped in to make coffee then headed off to do stuff I didn't ask about as I was trying not to be pushy and mostly failing, Vicky and I sat around going over and over things as we tried to find a way to do what we'd promised to do rather than get ourselves killed.

We drew a blank.

Ivan, in his wisdom, had asked us to do the impossible. He, or rather, Mikalus, wanted us to pull off the largest heist in history, and our mark was Cerberus itself. Mikalus, uber vampire with a grudge against Carmichael and thus Cerberus, wanted back what was his. All of it.

He wanted what he felt was his by right, everything taken from his library all those years ago. Hundreds of books of all manner and description, and it just wasn't possible.

Mikalus had done his research, had discovered what books were in Cerberus' care and which were out in the wilds so to speak, and so far, until I put a stop to it, I'd been chasing down those that had evaded Cerberus. I assumed when he got killed his staff had done what they could to hide some books, whisked them away somewhere, but Carmichael or whoever else was around at the time had taken most of the library and locked it away along with so much else.

Now Mikalus was in a position to reclaim what was his, and I was tasked with retrieving his collection. This went way beyond stealing books angels wanted back, which had caused me to stop working for him, this was on a whole other scale of madness.

But Ivan had told us things nobody else knew, had shared secret information and made it clear that however much it seemed like we were being given a good deal, this was personal, between me and him.

Sure, I could have said no, but I knew it would be bad if I did. They wouldn't let it lie, and Mikalus, nice as he'd been so far, was, when you got right down to it, the original vampire.

I cursed ever getting involved in their business. Cerberus was to blame for that. They'd tricked me into stealing his ashes, so this was all their fault. And this was the real reason why I agreed. Not because I was afraid of the vampires, but because Cerberus had it coming. They'd put me in an impossible situation by getting me involved in this whole sorry mess.

It was them who'd caused Mikalus to be resurrected because of their own greed and obsession with his ashes. It wasn't my fault the vamps were on their case and took them for themselves to resurrect their leader. Okay, maybe a teeny-weeny bit, but what's a poor wizard to do?

So this was about revenge for me, as well as Mikalus getting his revenge too. I wanted to rub Cerberus' face in the mess they'd created, and this was the perfect way to do it. I'd steal the books from right under their noses and they'd have to suck it up. I'd be free of the vampires, owe them nothing, and sure, it would mean the Hounds would be baying for my blood, but if I played my cards right I'd have a bargaining chip to make absolutely certain they never came near me or mine ever again.

All I had to do was figure out how to do it, and so far I had a big fat nothing. Oh, I had one thing. A very bad headache.

Hours later, after a crap sandwich, way too much coffee that sent me dashing for a pee every half hour, and with Vicky being Vicky, but a distilled, even more annoying version, after trawling over the obviously fake plans for the building Vicky unearthed, looking at aerial satellite imagery, going over what we remembered from being inside the building and the warehouse itself, and any other information we could get our hands on, I finally leaned back, laced my hands behind my head, and groaned, utterly exasperated.

"We can't do it," I said.

"Why not just use the Teleron and jump right in?"

"That's what Ivan thought I'd do, but it won't work."

"Why not?"

"Vicky, we've been over this. They've got that fucking scrubber, a magical scrubber. It stops magic working. You know that, you were there."

"That's to stop you using magic to get through the door, and to stop the artifacts giving off too much magic, not to stop you suddenly appearing right there in the room."

"You sure about that? You sure that if I used it, jumped right there into the warehouse, that the scrubbers and the disruption they cause wouldn't make the sudden appearance of a magical device go a little wonky? That I wouldn't end up scattered around the Nolands in a billion parts and that my hat wouldn't be ruined?"

"Um, not a hundred percent, no."

"There you go then. And besides, even if it did work, how the fuck am I supposed to find all his books? And there's bound to be guards inside. Sure, I could deal with them, but those scrubbers are the real concern. I felt it, they put a damper on any magical artifact in the warehouse, and if the Teleron goes wonky then I'm screwed."

"Fine, so what are we going to do?

"Find another way."

Beautiful silence descended, and for half an hour we were lost to our own thoughts, racking our brains for a way to pull this off. It was madness, it was Cerberus HQ and no way could we do this.

Then I had an idea.

No Time Like the Present

Vicky sat in silence—praise be—while I laid out my tentative plan, formulating most of it as I spoke. The more I talked, the more I got excited and convinced it just might work. Maybe. And if not, then let no man or beast say that The Hat hadn't tried his best to do the impossible.

During the whole time, Vicky remained motionless, back ramrod straight in the chair, looking like a gnome perched on a mushroom with her favorite tight red sweater, her hair pinned back so tight she looked like she'd had a cheap face lift, and her little pert nose scrunching up and wriggling about as if it had someplace else it would rather be.

"And that's how we do it," I said with a final flourish. Then I leaned back in my chair, folded my hands over my belly, and grinned at her, waiting for the praise to be heaped upon the master of thieves.

"Hmm," she mumbled, eyes downcast, suddenly finding the scrubbed table of interest. I say scrubbed, it still had traces of felt tip pen all over it where the girls had "accidentally" missed their paper, even though I'd provided them with the largest sheets I could possibly find. Not that I was bothered or anything, but I decided I'd treat myself and buy a new one.

I felt deflated, and then annoyed, as since when did I let Vicky make the decisions? I was the mastermind, she found out the info and then proceeded to get in my way and mess my plans up. But this was different. She was properly involved, as much a part of this as I was. Why? Because the vampires had asked specifically for her to be a part of this, and I guess that was because they knew we were a team. Not just that though. For all her nonsense, her drama, and her pint-sized peculiarities, she was smart.

"Haha, got you." Vicky's eyes suddenly flared like supernovae, body animated, and then she poked out her tongue and smiled. "It's so mad it might actually work."

"You think?"

"Yes, I do. So, if we're going to do this, let's do it. Can you get everyone together, so we can do this today?"

I thought for a moment, wondering if that was possible, then grinned back at her, and nodded. "I'll try my best. There's a lot to do though. You'll have to pull off some crazy things if we're to get away with this. Your skills up to it?"

"Arthur, I may have had a few issues recently, but I'm still one of the best hackers in the country. I can access anywhere, do anything. Just tell me what you need and I'll get it done. Oh, but I'll have to go get the girls, get a sitter." Vicky considered her options, then said, "Actually, maybe George would do it. I don't trust anyone else with them, not yet, and all my so-called friends, those bitches, have hardly called since Harry. Nobody comes around. They left me alone."

"People can't handle things like that. Nobody knows what to say or do, so they stay away," I said, knowing it hurt but that it was also understandable. But mostly knowing they'd never been her friends in the first place and she was right, they were bitches.

"Maybe. Anyway, will she?"

I called George and she promised to pick the girls up later from school and take them home to their posh pad. That gave us the whole day, and night, to get this done.

Were we being overly optimistic, thinking we could get all of this done in a day?

Yes, we were. But there was one very important thing I'd learned over the years when it came to stealing things and getting away with it. The faster you act, the less chance there is of being caught. Information always leaks, someone gets a hint of something and their guard is up.

People's suspicions become aroused by the simplest of acts, even if there are no snitches, and then you're screwed. If you want to nick stuff off other people, and you are involving anyone but yourself, then you'd best act fast or you'd find yourself either dead or worse. I'd had both of those things happen, and wasn't in the mood for a chat with Death or being caught by Cerberus.

Plus, Vicky had to get deep into some dark stuff online, and no matter how good she was there would be a virtual footprint, so we had to do this and do it now if we stood even a remote chance.

The adrenaline rose, we spoke fast and efficiently for the next half hour, and then, with Vicky clear on what she had to do until I returned, or called her, and with her fingers itching to get going and my wand tickling my leg in anticipation, I made us another quick sandwich, downed several cups of coffee, then left.

This was going to be awesome. It would also probably be a total disaster.

My Gang

I drove to the ruined, abandoned part of the city, then parked out of the way, hiding the car behind a crumbling brick wall covered in graffiti. Passing under flyovers with the hum of traffic above, it was like a different world down here. Dark, smelly, gritty, and real. I liked places like this.

Marshland was slowly spreading over the cracked concrete and taking over the canals and basins created to deal with water run-off because so much of the city was concreted over. Much of it was either low or dry because of the heatwave. Trolleys, bicycles, prams, and the detritus of a city peeked out above murky water, algae drying that hung from handlebars making it feel like I was walking through a weird mangrove swamp.

The heat was awful, the humidity high, and there were flies and mosquitoes swarming, which was something that had never happened before.

I passed the homeless, the high, and the hostile, but nobody tried anything. They all knew me, and they either nodded, smiled, or looked away, depending on how guilty they felt.

Eventually I came to the manhole cover I was looking for but always found hard to locate, and with a little magical help I got inside and climbed down into the sewers. The strong light was where I'd left it the last time I visited, so I hurried through tunnels both modern and antiquated and made it to Beast's lair in no time. I picked up the pipe beside the huge sluice gate, no longer used to contain water, and rapped in the right combination.

Huge chains rattled and grunts could be heard from the other side as the door lifted and heat like a furnace hit me, the stench of sweat and meat strong but something I'd grown accustomed to.

"Arthur?" said Beast with a frown. "You always come at night. You want to work out?" he asked, pumping away doing curls with dumbbells he'd fashioned from two scaffolding bars and a series of thick rusty cogs. He had the face of an angel and the body of a demon, and you did not mess with him, or even consider it.

"Nope, not right now. This is, ah, kind of a business call. I want you to do a job. With me, and Vicky, and, er, a few others." This felt awkward as I never, ever, under any circumstances, worked with anyone but my current partner. The more people, the more to go wrong.

"I'm retired," said Beast, then he turned his incredible frame away from me, his back so thick and wide it was like staring at some kind of genetically mutated superhero. Move over Hulk, Beast was the real thing.

"I know, I know," I said, trying to dodge the machines, the pulleys, the cables, the plates, bars, and other torture devices he used to build his spectacular physique.

"So why ask?" he said, suddenly turning back to me, looking genuinely interested. He took me off-guard as he so often did. Alfonse was softly spoken and kind-hearted, but a true man of violence and in his younger days, long before I was around, he had been someone to avoid at all costs.

"Because I need you, and I think you need me. You want some excitement, something to get you out of this cave and doing something worthwhile."

"Not interested." Alfonse positioned himself inside a contraption loaded with plates and slabs of steel and began pulling on a thick bar, drawing his elbows down and back. Apparently it was good for the back, of which he seemed to have several.

As he clanged and banged and grunted and the sweat streamed off his body, I waited patiently, and then, when he'd finished his set, I said, "It's to piss Cerberus off. I mean, really piss them off. This is the biggest job of my life and I'm freaked out, man, don't know if I can do it, certainly not alone. I need you, and you need this."

"Well, why didn't you just say so?" he asked as he untangled himself and strode over to me. He slapped me on the back, I tried not to fall, and he grinned widely. "Tell me all about it."

So I did.

One down, who was next? With a sigh, as I closed the manhole cover after laying it all out for Alfonse, I figured I may as well get the worst part of the day over with now, so it was with rigid shoulders, and ice in my heart, dread knotting my stomach, but my resolve unshaken, that I went to see a very annoying wizard.

Smelly and Hairy

I climbed the steps to Sisiminimus' loft, the smell of something I can only describe as what I imagine rancid tuna soaked in blue cheese essence then decanted into tubs of high octane jet fuel making it hard to breathe. Most of the smell would be emanating from a corner of the huge space above where piles of blankets, old paint-splattered canvases, and rags aplenty acted as a nest for an ancient, crotchety wizard.

He was also the best forger in the country, probably the world, and could make just about anything if paid enough.

Sure enough, as I stepped into the open-plan space, the walls once white now all the colors of the rainbow and others I was certain hadn't even been invented, loud snoring could be heard from the fetid corner. The pungent pile rose and fell rhythmically as Cousin It snored away, festering as he grew hairier and stinkier day after day, year after year.

Light streamed in through the high studio windows, the thick filth not enough to banish the sun on such a beautiful day. Sisiminimus seldom left his studio, liked to wallow in his sourness with only himself and the numerous artifacts cluttering the walls for company. They were piled up on various workstations, many partially assembled, or disassembled. It was impossible to know what was real and what was fake, and that was the whole point.

I sighed as I entered this strange world, wondered if there was another way, but knew there wasn't or I wouldn't be here, so strode over to the "bed" and coughed politely. The wizened wizard of yesteryear was grumpy at the best of times, and there never was a good time, but a bad one was when he'd just woken up.

No reaction, so I coughed louder, and then pulled back layers of rags stinking of white spirit, grubby blankets, sheets of unnatural color, and when I finally hit mounds of moldy clothes that looked like they'd disintegrate if I touched them, and I certainly had no intention of doing so, I saw his face peering out at me, eyes open and staring.

"Hi, it's me," I said with a smile and forced joviality that felt as sincere as a cat promising it just wanted to be friends with a mouse.

"Bugger off, I'm busy."

"You were sleeping."

"Like I said, busy."

"I've got a job for you," I sang, teasing the mini-yeti. "You're going to love it."

"Not interested, got loads of work. Busy year. And it's hot, and sunny, sleep until it's dark. Piss off."

Knowing I didn't have the patience with so much to do, and taking a real risk with my health and my life as the hairy wizard was prone to becoming murderous when treated with anything but utmost respect, I nonetheless grabbed a long stick covered in paint and used it to peel back the layers until a very naked, filthy, hairy creature that was somehow a man was revealed curled up and sucking on a strand of ashen hair.

"Hell, why don't you wash?" I asked, unable to stop myself. He was thick with the grime of years, maybe decades, his actual skin color impossible to discern. He was dark, like a wet pebble on the beach, or a toad hiding under a rock, which I guess was more apt, in the few places where the dirt wasn't layered too thickly, but most of him was multi-layered with paint, mud, specks of gold leaf, tiny lumps of metal that had merged with his skin, sawdust, wax, and I was sure things were crawling on him.

"Can't, I'll lose my power." Sisiminimus grabbed a handful of what looked like an old shirt and began to cover himself. It disintegrated in his hands. With a sigh, he sat up, rubbed at his eyes, then grabbed bunches of his long hair and yanked it behind his head. Strands fell and littered his bed; guess he really was building a nest.

"What, if you wash?"

The hairy Yoda scratched under his armpits. I gagged and had to look away. "Yeah, who knows what important stuff I'll lose down the plug hole? Could be gold between my legs."

"I don't think there's anything precious between your legs, old man, nothing anyone would want."

"Watch your tongue. Bloody kids today, no respect for their elders."

"And how old are you, exactly?" I'd always wondered, but the legend that was Sisiminimus was evasive, and his past was clouded in mystery, tall tales, and a hell of a lot of intrigue. He'd been employed by kings, chased by gods, and pissed off most everyone he'd ever come into contact with.

"Older than you. Help me up."

Reluctantly, and trying not to breathe, as he truly smelled like he had rotten tuna matted into his hair, I hauled him to his feet and took several steps back. He wandered off, checking on drying paper, moaning about the quality of fake diamonds, and generally avoiding me.

"Okay, here's the deal," I said, "and you're gonna love it." He ignored me, but I knew he was listening. If he thought he could earn, he'd be interested, no matter what he said. It was just his way. "I've got the biggest heist in history planned, the real deal, and to pull it off I need your help. But there's no time to waste, it's happening today with or without your help. If you want in, you can pretty much name your price. Cash or artifacts, and there'll be lots to choose from. We're stealing from Cerberus."

With that he dropped a bowl of something purple that hissed and spat then ate through the floor. He ignored it. As he turned, eyes wrinkled like prunes, he said, "Cerberus, eh? Well, if you're gonna screw with those fuckers then I'll help. Nasty bastards the lot of them. Especially that Carmichael."

"You know him?" I asked, shocked.

"Oh yeah, sure do. We got history. Long time ago now," he said dismissively. "But I remember. He deserves all he gets."

"You, er, know what he is?"

"Of course. A fucking twat."

"Oh, yeah, right." Guess the fact he was a vampire was a very well-kept secret just as Ivan had said. I wasn't about to share the information as I'd made a promise.

"So, you're in?"

"Just tell me what you want. But it will cost you. A lot." The wrinkled walrus in miniature rubbed his hands together with glee, and then we got down to business.

With everything set, I left and took a few minutes to get oxygen to my brain as I leaned against the wall in the alley outside, wondering how he could function in such an environment. But he would do as I asked, so it had been worth it.

The cost was astronomical, but he'd insisted it was the best he could do under the circumstances. The circumstances being that even if it gave him the chance to shove it to Cerberus he was still a thieving git and knew he could milk me dry. It didn't matter, Ivan had said he'd cover any and all expenses, plus pay out to me and Vicky an amount that was truly staggering.

All we had to do was survive.

Right, who was next?

More Old Wizards

Varela and Nohr were good guys. Traditionalists, quirky, and not to be crossed, which was how I liked my wizards, but without the pungency of Sisiminimus. They were also funny, always keen, and very excitable. The odd couple didn't get out much, didn't get involved in much of the magic world as it now stood. Both were from a different time and place, had values at odds with the up-and-coming generation, which I guess I did too.

They were powerful but overlooked, and that's a dangerous thing in a wizard. Many went off the rails when they got older, did stupid stuff, and often ended up getting themselves killed because they thought they had something to prove. These two had nothing to prove. They were content in their own mottled skins, happy to have been through so much and survived, and felt no need to push the limits just for the sake of it. So they were that rarest of things, old wizards with their marbles mostly intact.

Wizards have the ability to live extended lives, but most end up passing over not long after citizens because of the dangerous nature of magic and because of the kind of people attracted to this life of adventure and intrigue. It's wild, madcap at times, and very volatile.

As I knocked on the door to a small terraced house, I wondered how long I'd manage to live for. If it hadn't been for the extra lives gifted to me by Sasha then I'd have already been long gone, many times over, but I'd been more careful of late, hadn't got myself killed for ages, so who knew?

The door was opened cautiously and I looked down to see Varela staring at me shiftily. When he recognized me his face lit up and he shouted, "Arthur! You've come to visit."

"Thought it was about time. Can I come in?"

"Yes, yes, certainly," he said excitedly, opening the door wide to reveal a dark, narrow hallway that confusingly led right to the back of the house and an old glass door that was just clear enough to show a tiny patch of grass. Weird.

"Thanks." I stepped inside and he edged around me then closed the door.

"Nohr, it's The Hat. He's come to visit," Varela shouted, seemingly just into the corridor.

With that, Nohr appeared from out of the wall, the plasterwork sliding aside then closing behind him. Damn, that was one impressive secret door, I'd have to ask how they did it.

"Arthur! This is a surprise," said Nohr, pumping my hand furiously.

I smiled at them both, two wizened wizards you'd swear were brothers, then got distracted as something banged from the other side of the wall.

"Neighbors, eh?" I asked, unsure exactly where the rest of the house was, or what was going on. "How's it hanging, Nohr?"

Nohr pushed back his brown wizard's hood to expose a face hard to discern beneath the insane eyebrows, the beard and hair. So alike were this pair, it was hard to tell them apart unless you knew them well, but I'd known them for years so had it down pat.

"I'm Varela," said, er, Varela.

I glanced from one to the other, and Nohr pulled back his hood too, and I said, "Oh, right, sorry. It's the robes, and the beards. How you guys doing?"

"Great."

"Fantastic.

"Cool. Um, can we talk?"

"Sure, come in," said Nohr.

"I am, aren't I?"

"No, I mean in properly. This is just so the postman doesn't see what we're up to." He indicated the hallway.

"Oh, right. Okay then. Lead the way."

Varela walked casually to the wall and muttered something. A doorway opened and I was ushered inside.

"Wow, this place is huge."

"Nice, eh?" said Nohr.

"Awesome." I stood just inside, then turned as the door closed, only to find that from this side it was a wall of mirrors, not even a hint of it being a door. Then I turned back to the room, if you can call it that, and took it in.

"We keep it quiet, even the other side of the street don't know what we've done, but it's been like this for ages."

"Years," agreed Valera.

"Well, I'll be..."

"So you like it?" asked Nohr, seemingly keen that I did.

"I do. I really do."

We wandered away from the wall of mirrors and into a massive, long, single room the size of the whole goddamn terrace. Spaced evenly along the left-hand wall were doors painted different colors, the ones people would see from outside, and simple, discreet windows with various curtains, blinds, nets and the like, all very mundane. But they'd knocked every wall down between the houses, removed every staircase, everything.

I could see up to the apex of the roofs, strengthened with thick beams that looked like oak. The walls were smooth plaster and painted endless colors, the wood natural, the effect dizzying, inspiring, and utterly magical. It must have been four hundred feet long. There were even scooters, and skateboards.

There was a small kitchen alcove, a couple of rope hammocks strung up in the middle of the room, a single door which I assumed was for a bathroom, and everything else was given over to peculiar objects from countless countries. Large glass globes, quartz skulls, pitchers containing weird bubbling liquids, piles of what appeared to be sand, stuffed animals, antique furniture that tried to grab you as you walked past, pictures and paintings both abstract and so real the heads as well as eyes moved to follow you, and birds, brightly colored birds flying this way and that, landing on my shoulders and my hat then squawking and flying off.

There were nests in the rafters, some on the floor with wary birds eyeing me viciously, large eggs underneath them, and then I stopped dead and stared. "Is that a fucking Dodo?" I asked, pointing at, you guessed it, a Dodo.

"It is. We've got loads, do you want one?" asked Nohr hopefully. "They're greedy buggers and they keep stealing bits of my beard."

"Um, no thanks. Look, guys, I've come to make you the offer of a lifetime."

"We're in," said Nohr.

"When do we start?" asked Valera.

"Whoa! I haven't even told you what it is yet."

"Doesn't matter. We trust you, Arthur, and you know us, always out for a spot of adventure. What's the plan, eh?" He wiggled his eyebrows, great fat things that drooped down to his beard, and stared up at me with hope in his eyes.

They were always like this, loved to get into some seriously dodgy stuff, but this was keen even for them.

"We start right now, today. The job is going down tonight, and there are others involved. Don't worry, only the very best, and it's to shove it to Cerberus."

"Dirty buggers," said Nohr.

"Parasites," agreed Valera.

"So you're in?" I asked, knowing they were but feeling this should have taken a little longer.

"Fancy an egg?" asked Nohr.

"Um, I'll pass, but thanks. So, here's the plan."

It took a while, mainly because I kept getting distracted by all the awesome stuff, but we got there in the end. They knew what they had to do.

It was with a heavy heart that I finally left, as I could have spent weeks exploring their collection. Another time.

Maybe.

The Final Piece

This was a puzzle within a puzzle, a complicated, almost mind-bending trip through my repertoire of cunning plans and then some. This wasn't how I worked, ever. Vicky and me managed to screw things up just fine on our own.

But desperate times called for desperate measures, and this was something I couldn't hope to pull off alone. And besides, it would be fun.

By early afternoon I'd recruited who I needed, now it was time to put part of the plan into action. I called up Vicky and she answered on the first ring. I could just picture her sitting in my kitchen, coffee mug rings on my table, clutter and mess all around, staring at the phone whilst also typing furiously on her laptop.

"Hello?" she asked, like she didn't know it was me.

"Time to let it rip," I said, getting that familiar feeling in my belly, the knot of anticipation and excitement as the job began.

"Yes!"

I could picture her punching the air, and couldn't help but smile. Vicky really did love this stuff.

"You good to go?"

"You betcha, partner. This is going to be epic. You sure it will work?"

"No, but what choice do we have?"

"Then let's do it." I listened for several seconds, the sound of the keypad taking a beating, and then Vicky came back on the line. "All set. What now?"

"Now, my half-pint hacker, we wait. Keep me updated, text only, as I've got some stuff to do before the finale, but make it bad, Vicky, really bad. Throw everything you've got at it, and keep on doing it until they don't know what hit them."

"Roger. Over and out."

Vicky hung up and I smiled a nefarious smile.

Fucking Cerberus. They had this coming.

Bad Choices

I headed back into the city center and wandered aimlessly, wanting the closeness of strangers if not their actual company. On a whim, I called Steve, as we'd been seeing a fair bit of each other lately and I knew he was fed up after losing the work he'd assumed would be a regular thing. The rich dude he'd been working for had met a rather untimely end, and Steve, who hadn't been to blame, had been down in the dumps ever since.

I also realized that there was something missing from my plan, and he just might be the person to fill that gap.

He was keen for the company so I headed off to a pub to meet him and stood outside, cursing the heat, as I eyed the smokers reveling in their addiction, grateful for the nice weather so they didn't look like the sad gits they did when it was hammering down and they huddled together to satisfy their cravings.

I gulped nicotine-tainted air and waited for Steve, but he wasn't long.

As I saw him coming over the bridge then waiting to cross the road, I nipped inside and bought him a pint of lager and me a coffee. I was off the booze, not that I was ever a big drinker anyway. Magic and alcohol are way too potent a combination.

I grabbed a free table in the sunshine and sat, waiting for him to cross. He looked antsy, tapping his foot and constantly glancing left and right in between checking for the green man to start flashing, then hurried across the road, looking furtive and stressed.

"Man, this traffic's gonna kill me. It stinks."

"Nice to see you too," I said. "You wanna go inside?"

"Nah, it's better out here, mate. Get a clear view. That for me?" he asked, eyeing the lager greedily.

"Yep, sure is. And what's up? You look like someone's after you."

"Just the usual," he said with a shrug. Steve sat, took a long pull on the pint, which visibly relaxed him, then seemed to remember he was meant to be stressed. He glanced around, making me feel edgy too. He ran a hand through his freshly cut and styled in a disheveled way, hair, and smoothed down his waxed beard. He was typical Wild One in his fashion, and it suited him perfectly. He looked rugged, handsome, well-groomed, but manly too, although I wasn't as jealous as I used to be, probably because of the night I'd had.

"Come on, what's going on? You been up to something?" Steve, like most shifters, made a living doing dodgy stuff for people dodgier than himself, so there was usually something happening. I couldn't help but wonder if his problems were tied with what had gone down at Candy's yesterday.

"Ugh, I don't want to talk about it." Steve drained most of his pint then sank low in his chair, looking frazzled.

"You sure? You look like you do." I knew Steve, and one thing he was not, was good at staying quiet.

I waited him out, just sipped my coffee, watching the cogs turn, him weighing up whether or not to tell me. It took all of ten seconds.

"Okay, but you have to promise not to tell Candy."

"Damn, that's a big ask. You know we've been seeing each other for a while, and it's getting serious. I think. Last night, she, er, we, um..."

"Ooh, nice going, dude. She's totally out of your league, you know?" Steve grinned in that cheeky way he had, but he was just messing.

"Yeah, so I keep being told. Anyway, if this is about her, then I can't promise I won't say something. If I think she needs to know, that is." I wanted to be honest, and even debated telling him about the attack at the cafe, but it wasn't my place to talk about her business. What Steve said was up to him, I had my own set of rules I lived by.

"Okay, guess if you have to tell her then you do. But look, mate, just tread carefully. Candy's volatile, and she's smart, and she knows people, if you know what I mean?"

"Not sure I do."

"She's an important figure in our world, at least in this city. And you know we have our enemies, that we get involved in some dicey stuff."

"Don't we all?" I said.

"Haha, yeah. Remember when we met in that alley, you being chased, me saving your ass?"

"I could have handled it. And if I remember correctly, it was your fault anyway."

"Bollocks. Anyway, things are heating up. There's been some trouble, other Wild Ones trying to take over the business we usually do. Bodyguard stuff, a few other things, and I've had a few weird calls today. People accusing me of offing a few lowlifes, causing trouble, and their boss ain't happy."

"So you've got a turf war?"

"Mate, you don't know the half of it. Neither do I. These new ones, they're not like us, they're... odd. That's it, just odd. There's something about them that doesn't sit right, that freaks me out, and I've seen plenty of freaky in my time."

"What's this got to do with Candy beyond the obvious that it's messing with your business?" I asked. "Why don't you want to tell her this?"

"I haven't got to that yet. Candy's been acting secretive, there's something going on. She's hiding things from me, from all of us, more than usual. Look, I know she's smart, and a good leader, but there's something else. I hate to say it, and she'd kill me if she knew I said this, but watch your back."

I could have dismissed this as him being paranoid and worried about whatever in-fighting was going on, but I knew Steve and he was very loyal. If he thought Candy was up to something then he wouldn't have come to such a decision lightly. "Okay, I will. But come on, man, she's on the level. What do you think is happening?"

"I have no fucking idea, and that's why I'm saying. Candy's acting strange and all this crap we're dealing with is tied to it. She's denying it, not that I've pushed it. It's nothing obvious, but something is up."

I came so close to telling him about the fight, but something stopped me. I felt bad for not sharing when he was unburdening himself, but it would only stress him out more. That's what I told myself, but really it was because I didn't want anything to spoil what Candy and I had going on. Steve had already put the dampers on my happiness, and I didn't want to make it worse by having a drawn-out discussion about who the guys had been and any more conjecture about what it all meant.

I changed the subject, told him about what I had planned, and he instantly became animated. This was what I'd been hoping for, that he would be interested in a job, that he could get a crew together at short notice and help. Why hadn't I asked Candy to be in on this? Because it was dangerous and I didn't want to be responsible if anything went wrong. Would she be pissed off? Probably. Would she still be alive at the end of this day? Hopefully. And it wouldn't be my fault if she wasn't.

My stomach flipped when I thought of her coming to harm. Damn, I was falling for her in a big way.

I got Steve another pint and when I returned I sat and said, "Okay, so here's what I want you to do."

And So It Begins

I left Steve making phone calls and generally buzzing. He was out of his funk and keen to get involved in some action. Action that paid well too.

With the final arrangements made, I considered going to tell Candy what I was up to then decided against it. This was my business, not hers, and I didn't want her involved in it. Just because Steve and a few other shifters were, didn't mean I had to tell her.

But Steve's words kept going around in my head. Why was he suspicious of her? What was she up to? Just shifter business, I assumed, and she was dealing with the trouble in the best way she knew how. After all, she was in charge, sort of, and just like me and Vicky, not all information was necessarily shared. Steve was a great guy, but he wasn't the sharpest pencil in the case. He liked living on the edge, getting into mischief, but he wasn't much of a planner or a thinker. He kept his life simple and it suited him just fine.

Candy was different. She led her small group because she could plan ahead, so it made sense she didn't always share information.

Hell, who was I kidding? I had to tell her what I'd asked Steve to do, as otherwise it would be like I was keeping secrets. And as I came to this realization, I discovered that I'd been walking to the cafe anyway. As I got there I saw Candy outside, turning the key in the lock and shutting up for the day. Was it that time already? Damn, I had to get a move on.

"Hey, can we talk?"

Candy whirled around and was in a fighting stance before her mind registered it was me talking.

"Whoa!"

"Damn, sorry, you startled me. I'm a little jumpy after yesterday." She pocketed the key then pulled me close and gave me a big sloppy kiss right on the smacker. Oh, it was nice, warm, and wet, and it made me forget my name or why I was here.

Candy released me and stepped back, studying me. "I thought we were skipping tonight?"

"That's what I came to talk to you about. I can't stop, got a lot to do, but I thought it best I tell you. Just so you won't get mad. Or as mad as you would if you found out later."

"Okay," she said warily. "So, spill it."

It all came out in a rush, not because I was nervous of how she'd react as such, but because I realized I'd been stalling and time was getting on. I had places to be, things to do, shit to organize. Hopefully everyone was ready to do this, but it wouldn't be much good if I wasn't there to actually get it done. I surprised myself with just how much of the plan I told her. Guess I was getting comfortable with coupledom.

This kind of thing was also new to me. I never had to explain myself to anyone, ask anyone's permission for what I did with my life, and this felt like that. Like I was asking, and The Hat didn't ask. Um, unless it was George, or Sasha, maybe Vicky. Haha, so deluded. I was controlled by women whether I liked to admit it or not.

"So, is that all right?" I asked after finishing telling Candy. Yeah, I know, lame on legs, that's me.

"Of course it is. Steve's not my minion, he can do what he wants. We sometimes work together, but I get it. You don't want me involved as it would be weird, right?"

"Right," I agreed.

"Then that's fine. But are you sure about all this? I know Cerberus have been on your back, but this? It's going to cause a lot of trouble, you ready for that?"

"Trouble's my middle name," I said, winking.

"Then go get 'em tiger."

So I did. After I gave Candy a kiss.

A Very Long Drive

"Will everyone please shut the fuck up?" I yelled, considering crashing the minibus just so I could have some peace. Right about now a nice chat with Death felt preferable to listening to another second of this bullshit.

People! Drive you nuts.

Nobody paid me the least bit of attention. Or, they did, they heard me and I knew it, but decided to ignore me and continue their bickering and nonsense.

Sisiminimus was arguing with Steve about why wizards were better than shifters, Beast was at the back pumping the portable dumbbells he'd loaded up, refusing to leave without them, even though I had to go and inflate the tires to a dangerous level to accommodate the load, and Varela and Nohr were just gabbing excitedly about being on a road trip. Their conversation seemed to involve a competition to see who could talk the loudest.

As if that wasn't enough, which it absofuckinglutely was, the whole vehicle stank. Even with all the windows down, a mixture of Beast sweat, decrepit wizard smell, and the overriding stench of rancid tuna and cheese emanating from Sisiminimus made me want to tear my nose off and poke my eyes out with skewers because they stung so bad.

Steve's band of Wild Ones, temporarily under his charge as he was the one who'd got the job, were comparing previous exploits, what they'd done, who they'd worked for, and such like, and they were incredibly annoying. I won't mention their names, as such is the way with secondary characters introduced late in stories, they were the ones who got killed first. So it would be a waste of time.

And me, I was stuck up front with something even worse than the menagerie of magically mental maniacs in the rear. Vicky.

She talked non-stop the whole drive, and it took hours. She went over and over what I'd said about it not being a good idea to live in such a large house. She stressed about the girls, banged on about how hard it was to get good staff, moaned about her brother and how she was worried about him, delighted in describing the girls' new school, whispered about the secrets Ivan had shared concerning vampires, and just to ensure my mind remained in a perpetual state of flux, with me hardly getting a single word in, she constantly tapped away on her laptop, moaned when she lost the internet connection, and kept shoving it in front of my face when the next part of my plan came together and the chaos escalated in the city where Cerberus made their home.

I have to say, that part of it went very well, better than expected. It was the only time I focused on what Vicky was saying, mostly I did my best to zone out but the unending drone of her voice bored into my head and once there I couldn't get it to leave.

The capital was in chaos. Cerberus HQ was the scene of an insane amount of activity, all generated by Vicky and the vicious rumors she'd spread via the dark web and good old-fashioned social media. Nothing like posting a load of utter lies online to garner an instant, disproportionate reaction.

Vicky had told lie after lie, claimed the people inside the building were up to all sorts of terrible things, from government conspiracies, which was true, to things too dark and nasty to repeat. She'd posted photographs. She'd given the address, she'd told people there was a rally to protest about the secretive operations directed from this place that caused untold misery worldwide, and spread more and more propaganda. By the time we were halfway there, the surrounding streets were packed with people shouting and protesting, police were out in force, many of the personnel inside had left, the heavy hitters would have definitely had an escape route just in case the building got stormed, and there were news teams everywhere.

There were aerial shots of the entire building as news helicopters filmed the chaos, revealing many Hounds hurriedly leaving under the cover of umbrellas and hoods to keep their faces hidden.

General staff were evacuated to jeers and some were even abused by the protesters, but nothing too serious happened.

The main thing was that we'd caused utter chaos, put Cerberus on the back foot, given them something to think about and deal with.

A distraction.

We'd have less to contend with, or I would, once the real plan went into action. Hounds would be absent, the building would be running in panic mode, and people like Carmichael and others of his station would be long gone, holed up in swanky safe houses somewhere in the city.

But I didn't need to hear about it every five minutes. Vicky shoved the screen under my nose once again, right as I reached for my indicator, and I swerved, almost side-swiping a lorry.

"Will you please shut that bloody thing down and let me focus on my driving?" I pleaded.

"But you wanted to know what was happening," moaned Vicky.

"I said keep me updated, not shove a bloody computer in my face and make me crash and kill us all."

"It's not a computer, it's a laptop."

"Whatever, same thing."

"Is not."

"Just be quiet."

"Arthur, you're so mean."

"So don't talk to me then."

"Why do you have to always be like that? I'm doing all this work and you're just horrible to me."

"Ugh," I grunted, wondering if random noises would make her stop talking. It didn't, and the rest of the journey was made with the van bouncing as Beast exercised, fumes making everyone sick, wizards shouting about beards, Sisiminimus and one of Steve's guys having an arm wrestle, and Vicky alternating between shouting at me, moaning, or crying.

Ivan had a lot to answer for.

Here We Go

I pulled up as close as I could get, which was several streets away in a city in gridlock. The clock was ticking and we were behind schedule but I wasn't panicking, as I'd known this would happen so had kept my own schedule private. Plus, Vicky was crap keeping time so I'd got into the habit of giving myself an extra hour so I could get jobs done without rushing.

With people marching past wielding banners, shouting about injustice and the poor defenseless Welsh, yeah, she'd even got propaganda about the Welsh being made to eat leeks, their national symbol, every Sunday or receive a hefty fine—people will believe anything—we if not blended in then didn't look quite as out of place as we would under normal circumstances.

The main thing was that we would be lost in a crowd, not the focus of attention, as even with us looking somewhat odd, definitely a bunch of misfits, there were just so many damn people that it didn't matter. With everyone out of the van, and the foul air of an overcrowded city thick with the stench of millions of bodies and even more vehicles, I finally breathed. It was glorious in comparison to the van, so I let the carbon monoxide sear my lungs and gathered everyone down a side alley so we could talk above the roar of the angry crowds.

"Does everyone know what they've got to do?" There were murmurs of agreement, a little bickering, but it seemed like we were good to go.

"Steve, you and your guys go first. Do your thing, then wait for Beast to play his part, then you go for it, and don't hold back. I want that building full of screams, understand?"

"Gotcha."

"Sisiminimus, you be ready the moment you see people running scared from inside."

"Don't patronize me," he grumbled, pulling what looked like half a boiled egg from a filthy pocket and stuffing it into his mouth.

I took a step away as rotten egg odor hit, and turned to Valera and Nohr. "You guys, you're with Sisiminimus, and I'm relying on you."

"This is going to be such fun," said Nohr.

"Such fun," agreed Valera.

"You bet it is."

"Vicky," I said slowly, regretting it already, "you're with me."

"Really? Yes!" Vicky punched the air then did her awful mom-dance, rolling her arms over each other and wiggling her hips.

"Stop it, you look like a doll in cheap clothes having a seizure." Vicky gave me the finger—so unladylike—then continued.

With a sigh, and knowing it would all go to shit at some point, but with no other choice, I said, "Let's go."

Vicky and I watched as they dispersed into the crowd, making their way closer to Cerberus HQ and the scene of what was to be the biggest crime ever committed in the magical underworld.

"Do you think they'll do it?" asked Vicky.

"You mean follow instructions, do as I asked, and succeed?"

"Of course."

"Not a bloody chance."

As if on cue, the screaming started. I raised an eyebrow and stared at Vicky. "Fuck, I expected them to last longer than that before they screwed up."

People ran past screaming about rabid wild animals running amok, dogs and badgers and the like, even a hyena, and it was confirmed. Steve and his Wild Ones, and they got the name for a very good reason, had got carried away as I knew they would and were already causing chaos.

It didn't matter, it was part of the plan, just not a part they were privy too. When they get excited they're prone to change in an instant, and this was something way more epic than any of them were used to.

"Come on, let's go watch the show."

"But they're dangerous," said Vicky.

"I know, but they should be at the building by now so we're safe."

I dragged Vicky through the crowds, some running away, most unaware of what was happening and still converging on Cerberus HQ to protest about the government spooks inside doing a deal with Europe meaning everyone would only be allowed to buy vacuum cleaners below a certain power. Sadly, and I kid you not, we didn't even have to make that one up.

Yeah, the world was already about as screwed up as it could possibly be. Fact is always stranger than fiction.

Close Encounters

It was absolute mayhem outside the building. The road was packed with protesters, some shouting through megaphones, rallying their supporters, other groups seemingly having just decided it was a good excuse to go raid their wardrobes for old fancy dress outfits. Everyone was jumbled together even though there were at least five separate protests supposedly happening, each trying to raise their banners high, gain the steps to the building so they'd get a prime spot on TV as camera crews jostled and announcers tried not to look freaked out as everything descended into a multicolored, chaotic carnival.

Wild animals roamed, snapping at the backs of people, doing no real damage but coming close, but as Vicky and I made it to the steps the animals all converged halfway up and Steve, currently a fat badger rippling with muscle, stiff bristles raised as the blood lust gathered strength, charged headlong into the building through the open doors.

We waited for several minutes while the rest of the citizens working inside rushed out in a panic, just the stragglers who'd been loath to leave their work. We could hear the screams and the cries; I hoped the shifters weren't hurting anyone. Steve had promised me that the guys he had were professionals, had the rare ability to control the wildness to a degree, and would only kill if attacked directly.

There were a few suited men and smartly dressed women loitering at the bottom of the steps. Maybe spooks, maybe Cerberus, maybe both. These would be the low-level grunts, nobody with any real power. The big players, along with the Hounds, would either stand their ground or have exited by other, more discreet routes.

On cue, Beast ascended, his presence ensuring people moved out of his way no matter how crowded it was. The fact three diminutive wizards trailed in his wake didn't hurt either. The stench of Sisiminimus was sufficient to clear a wide path on its own.

They ignored us as they marched up and into the building, acting like they belonged but looking out of place. We didn't do tweed, we did oversized gym wear or long brown wizard cloaks complete with hoods and staffs. No matter, all the tech was on the fritz so nobody was recording this, nobody could. This was something Valera and Nohr were expert at, having grown increasingly paranoid about technology over the years, and wanting to ensure their lives remained private. They could easily shroud their presence from anyone who was observing, including those close to them, the radius extending some thirty or forty feet like a blank spot of blurriness.

Vicky and I fell into line behind this unlikely posse, gagging and urging as we were downwind from Sisiminimus. But we followed regardless, went right into the building and headed straight for the screams.

I'd laid out the floor plan as best I could, pieced together from footage we'd obtained from the lobby and what we'd seen when we'd entered last time. It was hard to believe we'd actually been invited, before our rather hurried escape after things went to shit through no fault of our own.

I shouted directions as we got closer to Beast, and soon we were at the inner part of the building. I recognized the door that led to the inner quadrant where there was a large lawn and space for a helicopter to land.

As the shifters came and went, the accessible halls and rooms cleared so no citizens were inside, we sped up and made our way slowly but surely through the inner sanctum of Cerberus itself.

It didn't take long for the Hounds to appear. It took even less time for them to be disposed of. In fact, it was a competition to see who could get to them first. No sooner had we turned a corner and a Hound appeared, gun raised or fist coming straight at someone's head, then either a dog, badger, or whatnot would attack, Beast would simply smash them aside and break their skull, or Sisiminimus would cackle and blast them with one miniature weapon or another, of which he seemed to have an endless supply. Even

Valera and Nohr got caught up in the violence, performing the occasional zap with a staff.

I didn't have to lift a finger, which made a nice change.

We made good progress, descending though the levels with hardly a hiccup, the most worrying part being stuck in an elevator, squashed in tight because of Beast's size and with the red, bloodthirsty eyes of our wild companions staring at me like they wanted some Hat for a snack.

Down at warehouse level, we jostled our way out of the final elevator, and boy was it a relief. My throat burned, my eyes streamed, and the nausea rose as we paused in the plain hallway.

This was it, we were so close now, and if this continued to go like it had then we were actually going to do this thing, succeed against all the odds. Now it was time to put the guys into action, to do what they'd come here for, so I went over the rest of the plan one more time even as everyone grumbled and the Wild Ones paced around excitedly, a very effective, and deadly, lookout team, and why they were so valuable to this operation.

"Okay, let's go." I strode down the corridor, coattails flapping, hair flowing behind me, wand in hand, feeling awesome and dangerous and itching for a fight.

I was followed by Beast, lumbering and sweaty, then three wizards of vast experience. A pack of wild animals darted to and fro, checking the coast was clear as we closed in on the warehouse and all the goodies it contained.

Wizard paradise awaited.

Doors Schmoors

I focused, as the last thing I wanted to do was get lost at this point, but I needn't have worried as the Wild Ones led the way, running off then returning moments later, bloodied and baying, the bodies they'd attacked a sure sign we were heading in the right direction.

Down corridors, around corners, and then, without fanfare, we were there. I stopped and held up a hand to signal everyone should do the same.

"Time to change back, Steve," I said to him and his pack. The badger nodded and did as we'd agreed.

As he cracked and the fur receded while he was on all fours, Beast pulled out a small bag with Steve's name on it and he took it, dressing gratefully in the clothes each shifter had in reserve.

The others were loath to change, to return to human form, and I understood the reasoning but this wasn't the plan, not what we'd agreed on.

"Tell them to do it," I said to Steve, annoyed as now wasn't the time to have them running about. We had to focus, be controlled, as what came next was the hardest part of all.

"You heard the man, time to—" Steve ducked as gunfire echoed in the corridor.

Valera threw up a shield and the translucent, almost jelly-like substance caught the bullets and slowed them until they dropped to the ground after squeezing slowly through the other side. But the animals were unstoppable. With lightning-fast reflexes, they darted after the Hounds, three men with machine guns standing cockily side by side in the corridor, firing continuously.

As I warned, Steve's pack were the sacrificial lambs in all this, their own fault but it was sad nonetheless, and they were mown down like the animals they currently were. The three creatures spasmed as the bullets ripped through their small bodies and skidded down the corridor leaving a slick, smeared trail of blood in their wake.

What pissed me off more than anything else, was that as the body of a mangy dog bumped into the leg of a Hound, he glanced down at it almost casually, sneered, then rested his boot on it and continued to fire. Such contempt for life was unforgivable. These dickheads were meant to be so concerned with all our futures that they kept the wonders of the world hidden away. Hypocrites.

Anger getting the better of me, I whispered into Valera's ear. He nodded then grinned at me.

"Wait here," I told everyone else. Valera and I advanced, the bullets still coming up short when they hit the shield. The closer we got, the faster the bullets came, though, and by the time we were five feet away, they were zipping through the plasma at a worrying rate.

"Now," I said quietly, and fair play to Valera, he dropped the shield without hesitation, although he did also drop to the ground himself, just as I'd told him to.

My wand burst into life, angry and deathly white as it fizzed like a sparkler on bonfire night, but a helluva lot more deadly. I shunted anger combined with will into this most precious wood, and as my hand arced right to left death was the result as a scythe of pure energy sliced through Hounds and cut them clean in half.

If you've never seen a body cleaved in two then don't go seeking such a sight, it gets messy. Guts and organs slumped from the top halves, blood spurted from the stumps, and then the bodies collapsed.

"Let's get this door open," I shouted as we ran back to the group. I nodded at Beast and he grunted in reply then joined me several feet away from the nondescript door that led to the scrubbing room and then to the warehouse itself.

I could have gone down the magic route, but I wasn't sure what would happen if I blasted the door off and the effects of the scrubbers escaped into the corridor, what I could only think of as some kind of decompression chamber. After Nathan's demise within the warehouse, there was also a very distinct possibility that the security had been beefed up and other nasty surprises awaited, so best save the magic for if, or when, it was needed and not risk harm unnecessarily. Last time I was here, when I'd melted the door this one replaced, the scrubbers had been disabled. I knew I wouldn't be so lucky this time.

Beast took a step forward as the rest of us took a hurried step away. He pushed his huge fingertips into the cracks around either side of the door and pushed deep, forcing the exterior wood to splinter under the pressure. Once his meaty fingers were up to the first knuckle, he tensed and simply yanked. The plain white wooden door snapped off with a crack. He threw it aside and puffed out his chest as he squared off against the steel, immensely thick and sealed tight so there were no magical leaks to get out of control, no scrubbers playing havoc with magic out in the corridor.

But we could all feel the magical emanations the scrubbers barely controlled, residues of magic that had built in the air for decades if not hundreds of years. Lingering, faint yet now part of the fabric of the building itself.

The door looked impossibly solid, and I wondered if we'd be better off letting Vicky try working her own unique brand of technical magic to try to get us in, but she'd been dubious about it, said that from what she'd seen the system was too complex for her to handle in a reasonable time period, so brute strength it was.

Beast stared at the door long and hard, as if weighing up an opponent, and then he slid his right leg back and with his not inconsiderable weight and immense power, he drove forward with his fist, pushing all his might into it. The steel thudded dully, dented but holding firm, so with a grunt he repeated the action over and over.

As the sweat ran down his bunched back muscles and he tensed, the muscles like knots of rope, every fiber visible, Beast took a different approach and began shouldering the steel.

Over and over, harder and harder, punching, battering, ramming, kicking, and just running straight at it, he assaulted the steel until every inch was covered in dents. The steel itself was unbreakable, that was the point, but it was put there, and held in place, and the damage was becoming evident. Around the door, cracks began to appear in the wall. Dust fell after each assault as the plaster and mortar fell away.

Then the wall disintegrated in earnest and long lengths of steel embedded in the wall became visible. Beast grabbed one and bent it like it was made of rubber, then methodically worked through several more until finally, with a monumental effort, he pulled hard on two rods, bending them back towards us in the corridor, and the whole doorway yanked away and fell with a loud clatter to the floor.

"Now you've just got to do the other one," I said with a smile as Beast turned to our applause.

His shoulders hunched as if in defeat, but then he raised his head and looked at me with his gentle eyes and said, "This is what I call a workout." His grin widened as he stepped into the scrubbing corridor. White light intensified and a humming grew louder.

The scrubbers were activated, negating any magic, but they hadn't been prepared for Beast. With an almighty roar, him somehow knowing where the scrubbers originated, he slammed into the wall and smashed right through the block work. He reached into a dark hole and sparks flew and things hissed then the lights went out and the humming ceased.

"That's a serious design flaw," I noted to Vicky, who ignored me and just stared at Beast in mute wonder as he went to work on the other door. I didn't have the heart to tell him I could blast it now, he was happy in his work.

But whatever he'd done to the first door, or maybe the scrubbers, must have short-circuited the wiring, and after a few hard knocks the door hissed. He jumped back, surprisingly agile for such a monster of a guy, and the door slid open, revealing the darkness of the unlit warehouse.

"Time to get what we came for," I said happily as we all joined Beast.

Everyone chattered at once, excited, and probably surprised we'd made it this far. I know I was.

"Be careful, there's a bloody big drop," I warned, as the lights flickered into life. "I'll go first, don't want anyone else getting killed."

Nobody argued, and I shuffled forward cautiously, stepped through the doorway, and stared out at the vastness of the warehouse.

All I could say was, "Uh-oh."

I Hate Him

Everyone crowded in behind me and we walked forward to the railing, unbelieving. I knew in my heart that what I was looking at, or what I wasn't looking at, was no trick, no Cerberus magic. This was real.

The enormous warehouse was empty. The endless racks were bare, the lights stark, shining on a polished concrete floor with nothing to see but tape and packing material.

And one more thing. Beneath us, staring up, dressed in a smart tweed suit, hair freshly cut, back ramrod straight, was Carmichael.

He smiled at me, then winked. Then he stepped backward through a rectangular portal and was gone. The portal snapped shut behind him and we were left alone in an empty warehouse.

"I despise that man."

A Depressing Exit

I was too stunned to do anything but get us out of there as fast as possible. We retraced our steps, fled as though being chased. The place was deserted. Nobody tried to stop us, shoot at us, or even look our way. Back up at ground level there were people returning to the building. Men and women in smart suits, others dressed casually, all of them looking annoyed at their work being interrupted. Security guards were in the lobby, checking people's credentials, but nobody paid us any mind as we left after Valera raised his veil again and we were nothing but a whisper, ghosts in a broken machine.

Outside, we stood at the entrance at the top of the steps and watched the protesters slowly disperse, their actions having finally been curtailed by a large police presence. There were lines of them across the street, erecting barriers and marshaling those who refused to leave into vans or frogmarching them to the other side of the barriers where some jeered and shouted but most shrugged their shoulders and made their way home or to the pub to discuss their activity.

We all just stood there, a bunch of magical misfits at the steps to Cerberus. I felt like a fool. I'd been duped by Cerberus, maybe by Mikalus, certainly by Carmichael.

Speaking of which.

A familiar movement caught my eye and I focused on a figure on the second-to-last step from the road, picking lint from his jacket as he watched the crowds leave. He turned, sensing my gaze, and our eyes locked. It was so affected, but he and I both knew this was staged. Heck, I'd just seen the man a few minutes ago. This guy definitely had a flair for the dramatic.

Carmichael stared at me, and only me. He shook his head, as if in genuine sorrow, then he slowly ran a hand across his throat, telling me in no uncertain terms that I was a dead man.

Fuck.

No More Fun and Games

Nobody bombarded me with a ton of questions, nobody moaned about us not getting what we'd come for. Nobody said a thing. I think they were as much in shock as me. We'd been so hyped about this, focused on what we were after, and my head was consumed with my plan, about how we'd get in, but more importantly get away. Now that part of the plan was lost, useless, never to be implemented.

Such a major disappointment. I didn't even know where to begin to get this figured out. Yet in one way it needed no figuring out as it was blindingly obvious for all to see what had happened.

Cerberus had emptied the warehouse, moved artifacts collected over centuries somewhere else, and we hadn't stood a chance from the get-go. They'd been one step ahead of us the entire way and now we were screwed. Or I was.

This was all on me. I was to blame, I was the ringleader, I was the one running this operation and I was going to take the fallout.

I'd had it all figured out, too. I would have got Mikalus' books and taken quite a load of extras too, giving myself a way to negate the backlash. They wouldn't lay a hand on me as then they'd never get back the things I'd stolen, and although it would rankle that I'd taken Mikalus' books it wasn't like I would have cleaned out the whole warehouse.

But none of that had happened, and I was screwed.

From the high of being deep in a job, to the low of coming away without a thing to show for it apart from several dead shifters, the comedown was extreme. Sisiminimus hadn't had chance to play his part, and it would have been awesome, and everyone else had fairly major roles to play, had prepared and were geared up for it. I felt like I'd let them down, that I'd disappointed them and there was no prize after all our hard work.

Unable to stand the silence a moment longer, I took a turn at a service station and pulled off the motorway. After I parked up, the van still silent, and not knowing what else to say, I unfastened my seatbelt, turned to the back and said, "I'm sorry."

"Those bastards," muttered Sisiminimus.

"It was still fun," said Nohr.

"A fun excursion," agreed Valera.

"That door was a worthy opponent," said Beast with a gentle smile.

"Shame about the lads," lamented Steve. "But it was how they would have wanted to go out. They always were a bit wild, never listened. Haha."

"You guys are the best, seriously. I'm so sorry. This was meant to be epic, us giving Cerberus the finger, but they screwed us, saw us coming, and I want to know how."

"Chin up, mate," said Steve. "They obviously cleared the stuff out ages ago. They were just messing with you."

"No, I would have known. This is recent, very recent. After, er, something happened last year, they had every opportunity to empty the warehouse. Vicky and I were there, they knew we knew what was inside, but they did nothing. No, something's going on. They knew, but only in the last few days."

"That means it's close, right?" asked Vicky, hope still in her eyes.

"Maybe, maybe not. But it doesn't matter, this is over now. We'd never get it, not with them on the alert. We wouldn't stand a chance. Nope, this was our only opportunity and we blew it. I blew it. Look, you'll still get paid, I'll make sure Ivan keeps his promise and everyone gets what they deserve."

"Don't sweat it, mate. It happens. Not every job is a success and sometimes you have to cut your losses."

There were murmurs of agreement from everyone, even Sisiminimus, who, for all his crotchety old man mannerisms, knew how the game worked same as everyone else. It almost brought tears to my eyes, it really did. Who ever said there was no honor amongst thieves?

"Thanks, all of you. Come on, let's get going."

I buckled up, joined the motorway again, and headed back to our city where we could all go home, lick our wounds, and dream of what might have been.

How had they known? What was going on? I may not have known the ins and outs of what had happened at Cerberus HQ but something told me that there was a lot more to this story than I'd been led to believe. Mikalus had eyes and ears everywhere, he would never have sent me if he'd thought the warehouse had been cleared out, so that meant only one thing.

We had a traitor in our midst. I didn't know how, or who, but it was the only explanation. Somehow, somebody had got wind of what I was going to do, maybe before I was even asked, actually, definitely as that was only yesterday, and they'd told Cerberus.

The realization made me very uneasy. This was the kind of crap I hated. All the skulking about, the secrets and lies, the politics and the wheeling and dealing behind closed doors, people playing their games, using us poor wizards as their pawns.

I was being used, had been set up, and as I mulled it all over on the drive home, I came to an understanding. I hoped against hope that I was wrong but knew I wasn't. But if I was right, if this had all been about what I thought it was about, then I wasn't just screwed I was utterly fucked. Up the ass, with a goddamn rocket. A big one, with sharp bits.

Welcome Home

I dropped everyone off, which took ages as we're a secretive, paranoid bunch. These guys were some of the best in their respective fields so had more quirks and rituals they had to perform before certain actions than a bunch of nuclear physicists with professionally diagnosed OCD, so I had to take circuitous routes, switchbacks and what have you, then let them out at various random places throughout the city. It wasn't a fast operation.

Finally, we drove to Vicky's, the atmosphere tense, the vibe low, feeling let down and frustrated. A job incomplete gnaws away at a thief, as though a limb has been removed.

The girls were in bed, George was watching TV, so we filled her in on what had happened while we ate leftovers she'd defrosted from the freezer, and as we drank coffee, she sat and thought for a while. George was super-smart, way smarter than Vicky and I. A different generation of magical user, where brains were just as important and got as much training as the esoteric. Plus Sasha had been putting her through her paces, teaching her all about the fae, and the fae may be sneaky and untrustworthy but they were intelligent like you wouldn't believe.

So George let the information filter through, weighed up all that had happened, and said, "Don't be surprised if you get a call soon."

"I know, Mikalus is going to get Ivan to phone and give me hell. He'll be certain there's a snitch too. He'll have figured it out, that someone told. Maybe one of their guys, it has to be. He's going to blame us for not knowing, not finding the new location and getting what he wanted."

"Man, you are dumb at times," she said, looking from me to Vicky.

"Hey, we did our best," protested Vicky. Me, I did feel dumb.

"You really don't get it? Either of you?"

George sighed, like she was talking to two children. "You're going to get a call from Carmichael."

"What, to rub our noses in it?"

"No, to go mental at you for stealing all of Cerberus' goodies."

"But we didn't," said Vicky. "We told you, the warehouse was empty."

"Guys, come on, can't you see what's happening here? You've been used. Set up by Mikalus."

"Okay, now I'm really lost," I said. "Take a step back, explain it like we don't know what you're talking about. Because we don't."

"You'll get a call from Carmichael," she lectured, "going nuts at you. He was at the warehouse, being all smug as they'd managed to empty it just in time. But he won't be feeling so smug now, as while you guys were there, Mikalus had someone else, probably his own people, intercept the artifacts, and they'll have them by now. My guess is he'll have all his books and plenty more besides. Maybe everything Cerberus has taken over the years. Mikalus set you up. He got Cerberus to move everything so he could take it. I bet it was en route somewhere and he hijacked it, fooled you, fooled Carmichael, fooled the real boss, whoever that is."

"Fuck, that bastard. Damn, you're right, Carmichael will go nuts. He'll blame me, think I was in on it. And I've got nothing, no bargaining power. No artifacts to give back if he promises to leave me alone."

"Yup, you messed up big time." George didn't say it to gloat, she was just stating the obvious. My daughter was a direct girl, didn't mollycoddle the truth. She was strong and powerful and faced up to the reality of the situation, be that good, or in this case, extremely bad.

"I can't even think about this now," I said, a deep weariness taking me over as the evening grew late. It was past ten and I wanted to sleep, or at least lie down and get stressed in a prone position. "Let's go."

We got our things together, I promised Vicky I'd call her in the morning and we'd get this sorted one way or another, and then we left.

George and I talked it over in more detail on the way home, and what she said made perfect sense. What better way for Mikalus to get the artifacts away from the warehouse than to plan a heist and let Cerberus know all about it? It was kind of genius. And he couldn't tell me as that would look fishy. Cerberus had to believe I would do it.

There were a lot of flaws in her reasoning though. We hadn't been given the job until the day before, and by that time Cerberus would have already moved everything, wouldn't they? George said maybe not, that they probably had systems in place to empty the warehouse at very short notice. Trucks and what have you standing by, which was why Carmichael had been there. He probably oversaw the removals and they'd just that moment finished, a rush job once they confirmed we really were going to attack. Maybe once they saw that I was recruiting, they'd sprung into action and moved everything?

Part of me wanted to believe George, because it made sense, but a big chunk of my gelatinous, decaying by the day, brain wanted to believe it was just a terrible mistake and I hadn't been played like that. Not by Mikalus. And what about Ivan? Had he known? Doubtful, as it involved Vicky, and he was a man of honor like me, so wouldn't stoop that low. But then, I found it hard to believe Mikalus would either.

By the time we'd gone through the portal, got home and parked up, my head was spinning and I wasn't sure of a single bloody thing.

We got out of the car and stood on the cobbles in our courtyard, our beautiful home and the sanctuary it represented right in front of us. Chickens clucked from their roosts, the pig snored, and I glanced at the barn where Marjorie had lived for so many years.

I missed the old girl. Who would have thought a donkey could mean so much to you? But she had, and I missed seeing her head with its large ears poking out over the barn door to see what was going on.

Still, it was home. It was ours. It was where we belonged.

My phone rang and I answered, wondering what kind of crap I'd hear and who it was. Carmichael or Ivan?

"You went too far this time, old chap." Carmichael sounded almost sad about it.

"I'm just as confused by what happened as you are," I said, which was the truth.

"Goodbye, Arthur." Carmichael hung up.

"That was weird," I said to George. "He sounded quite final about that."

George just shrugged.

At that moment we both looked up. There was a buzzing, or a humming, as if a swarm of bees was closing in on us, faint yet getting louder.

I knew the sound; it wasn't bees.

"Run!" I shouted, and I grabbed George by the arm and pulled her away from the house as fast as possible. I released her at the gate, launched over, yelling, "Get away from the house, now."

She didn't ask questions, just vaulted the gate and landed beside me. I grabbed her again as we ran for all we were worth across the lane and into the field opposite. I was panting already, close to hyperventilating, stumbling and panic-stricken, but I pulled on her harder and made her speed up.

For ten seconds we ran as the hum grew louder, and she shouted, "What is that?"

"It's a fucking drone strike," I screamed above the roar.

Then the world exploded.

What Number is This?

"That was fucking awesome!" said Imaginary Figure of Death, or maybe it was the real man himself, I never could get to the bottom of it all, not even now.

"Awesome?" I said with a groan, picking myself up off a pebble beach at the edge of the eternal waters where Death liked to hang out and stand silently watching the waves lapping gently at the shores of time itself, contemplating his navel and sharpening his scythe.

"Awesome!?" I continued. "Are you nuts? I just got blown up by a fucking drone strike. Oh, no. George, is she...?" I couldn't even bring myself to say it, but I had to know. "Is she dead?"

Death looked down at me, or I assumed he did. His cowl shifted but the impenetrable darkness held no sign of a face, no eyes gleaming with menace and insight into my soul, just emptiness. "Hmm, now let me see. Where did I put the ledger?"

Death glanced aside and a simple small table was suddenly there on the beach, complete with plain wooden chair and even a quill and inkwell, plus the biggest bloody book you're ever likely to see. Trust me, you do not want to see this book. It was infinite, huge, and thick. Ancient, and with pages thinner than a Hollywood star's facial skin. He did like his parlor tricks.

Death glided over and sat down, licked a bony finger, and I mean bony, then flipped through the pages. Wafer-thin pages that turned without him touching them, covered in names in tiny, spidery handwriting. Not that I could ever read any of them, that wasn't allowed. For his eyes only.

"Ah, here we are," he said jollily, while I tried not to lose my mind. "George. Hmm, nope, she's good. Well, I say good, um, well, now this is a rather strange thing."

"What is?" I asked as I clambered to my feet, having found that I'd collapsed under the stress, and wandered over.

Death snapped the book closed and turned to me. "She isn't mortal. Why'd you ask me if she was dead?"

"Er, because everyone dies, don't they?"

"Arthur, please, you should know by now that I'm not your bloody teacher. But she's fae, and they have... how shall I put this? They have their own way of doing things."

"Oh, right, so she's not on your radar then?"

"Never will be."

"So, is this it?" I asked, "Is this my final life?" I crossed my fingers behind my back, praying I had another chance, because if I did I was gonna destroy

Carmichael, Cerberus, and Mikalus too for what he'd done. Angry, I blurted, "They fucking drone-striked my fucking house. With my fucking daughter there. Those fuckers."

"Language," warned Death. "And is that really a word, drone-striked? And, er, what is a drone? Is it like an imp, a devil of some sort?" Before I could answer, he continued. "Have you no respect for the one that sees every mortal soul through to what awaits? Who helps you transition from one existence to whatever comes next? Stop swearing, it's awfully tiresome. Rude too," he chastised, turning suddenly. The table, chair, and book vanished as he wagged a finger at me. I hated this shit, had no time for it now, not that it ever took any time at all.

"Sorry, I'm stressed. So, my lives? Is this it?"

"It should be, you're my worst customer ever, and I've had a lot."

A thought struck me then, and even under the circumstances I had to ask. "Hey, do you actually know what comes next? You sounded unsure, said you helped people from life to what came next. But do you know?"

"Arthur, I am Death itself, a physical representation of what you expect to see. To others I am something different entirely, all depends on your outlook, I suppose."

"That doesn't answer my question."

"No, it doesn't."

"Fine, be like that. Just asking. Can I go now? I'm kind of busy."

"Trust me, you don't want to go back, you're in a right mess. All that exploding of buildings, such destruction. I've said it time and time again until I'm blue in the face, or, um, slightly off-color anyway, that missiles shouldn't be allowed. Whatever happened to a good old poke in the guts with a bayonet? Those were the days."

"So you do know what a drone is?" I asked, beyond frustrated.

"Maybe I do, maybe I don't."

What was wrong with him? I swear he was smiling behind that cowl, almost like he was enjoying himself. Could Death get laid? Was he in a good mood?

"For fuck's sake," I screamed. "Is this even real? I want to know if you're Death or imaginary. I'm pretty sure I've died before, and this is what, number seven? Or eight? Uh, anyway, are you real?"

"Does this feel real?" With that, Death swung his scythe, the infinite blade slicing the air, cutting it, and with that the tip of my nose.

"Ow! Motherfucker! You cut off my nose."

"Don't be such a baby, it's just a flesh wound. And besides, you're dead. Yes, really dead, so how have you even got a nose?"

I put my hand to my nose, and it felt real enough, hurt like hell, but he had a point. "That's your department, not mine. Now, can I go or are you gonna send me off on a little boat to meet my afterlife, make me pay for my sins?"

"No, I don't do that any more, too predictable. And actually, you've done pretty well, your sins aren't worth much, hardly a footnote in history. I hate to say it, but you're one of the good guys."

"I very much doubt that," I mumbled. "I've killed, beaten, blasted, stolen, and done it more times than I can remember."

"As I said, you've been very good by human standards. It's not just about what you do, it's about what you think, and feel. In your heart you're one of the better humans. You should see the darkness in a lot of my clients. Ugh, gives me the shivers just thinking about it."

"Are you okay?" I asked Death. "You're acting weird. You seem very upbeat, like you're in a happy place. Are you on medication? Normally you get annoyed with me and tell me to bugger off, and then do something that hurts just to get back at me for being cheeky."

"Oh, haha, you noticed, did you?"

I swear he really was smiling, at least he sounded like he was. This was getting weird, or weirder, and I didn't even know if I was going to get to go home and check on George or not.

"Um, yeah, sure."

"I got a new scythe. Nice, isn't it?"

I rubbed at my nose. "It sure is sharp."

"Has to be. Gotta reap the souls with it, needs to be sharp enough for that."

"Oh, right." There was an awkward silence as we both contemplated his scythe, then it began to get uncomfortable. "Um, about my death? Can you send me back? Or is this it?"

"Arthur, you are blessed, my friend. Today is your lucky day. Off you go, but I'll be seeing you. Soon."

And with that, Death rotated his scythe, his new, very shiny and sharp one, and it somehow shrank to half size and the blade passed right through my middle. It felt real enough, like I was genuinely cut in two, and then everything was white and there was a loud ringing in my ears and I was flying through the air, still holding on to George as fire erupted, the air shook, and the world was nothing but roaring and buzzing.

My jacket burst into flames and then fell away, then I had the presence of mind to up the protection around us both, hoping it wasn't too late.

We landed with a thud in the parched grass, and lay there, somehow having landed on our backs. I looked into the sky and watched missiles trailing white vapor before they flared briefly, orange against the starry night, then angled down and exploded into my house that was already nothing but rubble.

My phone rang, so I answered.

"Hello?"

"Just checking," said Carmichael. "Shame, I thought you'd be dead."

"Me and Death have an arrangement," I said.

"Then you better get ready to meet him again." Carmichael hung up.

For a moment it didn't make sense, but then I looked up and saw a missile change direction, flaring briefly as it turned.

"Fuck, my phone," I muttered, and then I stared at George, who was groaning but already getting to her feet, and I ran not for my life, but for George's. They were homing in on my phone and this time they'd make sure they got me.

I ran for all I was worth, and then as magic welled inside me and I willed it to do what it could, the missile hit.

"Seriously?" asked Death. "It's been what, about ten seconds?"

"I missed you," I said with a grin. I got the terrible feeling that my luck had finally run out.

Not Again

Death walked away down the beach, the pebbles making a pleasing clattering sound even though he wasn't actually touching them. He settled himself haughtily at his table then went through the routine of licking his fingers before he swept the ledger open with a wave of his hand. He hunted through the pages and found what he was looking for, so I took the opportunity to go join him.

"Find anything interesting?" I asked, peering over his shoulder.

"Hey, no peeking," he said, slamming the book closed, but not before I saw the page.

I jumped back, unable to fully comprehend what I'd seen, but wondering how long my entry was.

Almost at the bottom of the page, after thousands upon thousands of other names, was my name, I was sure it was. Arthur "The Hat" Salzman, written repeatedly, one beneath the other. How many times I wasn't sure, but it looked like quite a few, and how many times was it written on the next page? Just how many lives did I have? What was this? Eight or nine? I lost count. But it looked like more than that, I was sure of it. Maybe the entries went on for pages and I had more lives than an immortal jellyfish.

I grinned at Death and said, "Guess you're not going to tell me how many times my name is written, are you?"

"Nope," he said glumly.

"So shall we forgo the nonsense and you send me back?"

"Fine," he said, sounding trite about my refusal to play his games.

"Hey, if it makes you feel any better, you're doing a great job."

"Oh, gee, thanks, that's made my millennia."

"Really?" I asked, feeling pretty good about that.

"No. Will you please just fuck off?" Death cut my head off, and he seemed pretty grumpy about it. Maybe something had happened in the interim, as he sure had lost his chipper mood.

I came to gasping in a ditch, face down in thick mud. I spluttered and clambered out, breathing deeply, and wondered where all my clothes were. Ah, the bomb, that'd be it.

Panicked, I reached for my head. Grace was still there; not even a bomb could destroy The Hat's hat.

But my wand, it was gone, incinerated along with my clothes.

It was at this point I remembered to throw away my phone, but it was already gone, along with so much else.

Somehow, I knew the thing I cared about the most would be okay, yet my heart still sang for joy as George came running over and hugged me tight.

"You okay, honey?" I asked.

"Fine. You?"

"My wand got burned up."

"And you got a bomb dropped on you."

"What, that little thing? It was nothing. I'm The Hat, it'll take more than a bomb to get me."

"Tough guy, eh?" said George, eyes twinkling, smiling at me. She was a good girl.

"You betcha. And they broke the Code. You never, ever, go after people's kids."

George nodded. She knew the rules same as we all did.

No matter what you did, what grudge you had against someone, however bad it got, you did not, ever, involve wives, partners, or children. It was our way, our Code, and Carmichael had broken it.

We shuffled back to the wreck of our home. There was nothing there, nothing left. It was gone, utterly destroyed. There wasn't even a fire, just massive craters in the ground.

All that remained was a chicken. And as we stared at it, lost in wonder about how it could have possibly survived, a flash of red came out of nowhere. A fox grabbed the chicken as feathers flew and ran off into the night.

"Typical. Bloody typical," I grumbled. Then I collapsed.

Gonna Be a Long Night

I didn't stay out for long, and I think it was more relief that George was okay than anything physical. Coming back from the other side always had a strange effect, the cause of death obviously gone, as otherwise I would have been strewn around the field in numerous hat-sized chunks, so in a way it felt like I'd been put back together better than before.

That was the physical side of it, but the mental? Not good. I had, after all, just been killed by an explosion, then more directly by a freaking missile, bomb, whatever it was. That's gotta mess with you psychologically. Nonetheless, I got up with a little help from George and we checked to see what we could salvage. But I was shivering and felt weary beyond belief to be wandering around a bomb site with just my hat on while my daughter tried not to stare at my scrawny ass.

It was a fruitless search, nothing but craters, dust, the odd brick or stone, and not a lot else. Our entire life had been obliterated. I bent, something shiny amid the dust catching my eye, and pulled out a mangled tap, the new one from the kitchen. I chucked it, no point having a tap without a kitchen.

And you know what? As I settled down, let the anger subside, it felt like a relief. There was nothing like a fresh start to make you look to the future, and this was as good a reason as any to move on. Not that we had any choice.

"Hey," I said, "where do you fancy living next?"

George turned to me, confused, but she caught the twinkle in my eye, the grin on my face that spread as we connected on the same wavelength and saw the funny side of it. What else can you do under such extreme circumstance except laugh at the world, and yourself?

"How about somewhere closer to the city? Not in the city, but closer. Or, how about a city house for a change?"

"No bloody chance, it's too noisy. No peace. Can you imagine how many people would come calling?"

"True. Okay, Wales?"

"Nope, been there, it's really wet."

"Scotland?"

"Even wetter."

"Fine, you choose."

"Hmm, I have always fancied a proper farm, something with a bigger house, and maybe some stables. But, oh, what would we do if we bought somewhere that had, say, paddocks and maybe stabling, and fenced-off areas and a large courtyard, larger than this one." I indicated the pockmarked ground, not that there was a courtyard there any longer.

"Stop teasing." George smiled as I played out the game, but she knew where this was heading

"Haha, fine. I know you want to have a business, do something to earn money. How about we get horses? You can do horsey stuff then."

"Equestrian, that's what it's called. Horsey! You mean it?"

"Sure, if you do?"

"Awesome! Thanks, Dad." And with that, the deal was done.

Yeah, we were a hardy pair. A missile strike was nowhere near enough to get us down. We saw it as an opportunity.

I was still going to go old skool on Carmichael though, and anyone else who'd played a part in this deception.

An Understanding

We trudged back to the barn where I dressed in clothes I had stored there for such events, although not quite as specific as a drone strike. I grabbed a spare phone and set up call forwarding from the old number, and then we headed through the portal. Neither of us felt like it was a great idea to stay in the house, so I called Vicky and she answered blearily after several rings and said we could come stay. I told her I'd fill her in when I got there.

I didn't think she'd be at risk, as although involved, it was me they were gunning for. And me for them.

This is the price you pay, Arthur, was something that did not go through my mind. Why? Because this was not what was meant to happen. There were unwritten agreements, honor and duty and respect of a sorts no matter how at odds you were. You did not endanger your foe's family, and even worse than that, you did not double-cross, treat your employees as expendable commodities. Carmichael and Cerberus were one concern, and I'd deal with them, but Mikalus, and what he'd done, that was different. That was unforgivable.

As we drove to Vicky's, the realization suddenly hit me.

I was at war with the vampires.

"Dad?"

"Yeah?"

George glanced at me nervously as I tried to stay focused on my driving even though I was fading fast now, closing in on myself after such an ordeal. "Nothing," she said.

"Come on, it's fine. What is it?"

"You won't give up, will you?" She looked concerned, like she was getting ready for a huge disappointment.

"How'd you mean? Like not buy a new place, get you the horses?"

"No, I mean stop doing what you do? Give up the life. The magic. The artifacts, all of it?"

I pulled over into a bus stop, they wouldn't need it at this time of night, then turned and looked my daughter straight in the eyes. "Why are you asking?"

"Because I know you, and I know you worry about me. I don't want you to give up what you love because you're worried about what might happen."

"Honey, it honestly hadn't crossed my mind. Yes, I worry about you, every moment of every day, and even more at night. I'm a born worrier, what can I say? But no, and it may sound awful coming from your father, but I hadn't even considered giving up. I know my work can be dangerous, and it has made its way to our home, which I am truly sorry about, but I won't give it up. I won't give it up unless you ask me to. I know how you feel about all of this, that you're like me, born to magic. It's dangerous, it's wild, and I hate that it puts you at risk, but this is who we are. Not who. What. We are wild, George, and dangerous. I'm a wizard and you will be an amazing witch one day, or faery, I guess. You're special. I don't even think you can be killed any more, Sasha certainly can't, so don't worry, The Hat will be getting into trouble even when he's old and decrepit."

"Haha, you mean like now?"

"Cheeky git!"

George smiled then leaned over and hugged me. "I'm glad. Don't ever change. I can't imagine you not running around like a nutter, getting up to all sorts."

"Neither can I."

And I couldn't. This was the truth of it all, of my life. This was who I was, who I would remain, and now I had a new purpose.

"Come on, let's go see Aunty Vicky and enter a world that's truly mad."

George grimaced and we both steeled ourselves for the sleepover from hell.

Lumpy Bed

Vicky had a million and one questions and wouldn't let us go to bed until we answered them. Not that there was too much to tell. I filled her in, explained to her and George about my meetings with Death, which they both always loved hearing about as it's not your typical everyday happening, and then she asked the most important question.

"So, what are we going to do about it?"

"That, my diminutive grasshopper, is easy. We're going to find out what happened, what really happened, as this is too big to deal with without as many facts as possible, and then we'll deal with everyone involved. Everyone. This has gone too far. They've overstepped the bounds, so it's crunch time, the real deal."

"Good. They made us their patsies," said Vicky.

"No need to turn into a gangster's moll," I groaned, despairing of her attempts to use gangster talk. "We'll start tomorrow, get the facts, figure out what to do. But right now I need rest. And George does too. Right?" I turned to George but she was curled up asleep on the sofa.

She looked beautiful, red hair spread on the cushions like silk, sharp cheekbones angling down to her full lips. It was at moments like this that I understood just how exceptional she was. She wasn't just a pretty woman, she was otherworldly, mesmerizing. Strange, and maybe even scary to those who didn't know her. But to me she was just my daughter, and that was probably the most terrifying thing of all. She was fae, had knowledge and skills no human ever would or could, and for as long as I lived she would be my responsibility.

Vicky got blankets for her, and George snuggled up without waking. I was shown the spare room, or one of them in this oversized house that I knew Vicky would last in for only a few more months before it all got too much for her. I showered in the guest bathroom, en-suite, very posh, crawled under the covers, and readied for a night of lying there stressing and trying to formulate a plan. I was one guy, stuck between Cerberus and the vampires. It had to stop.

Nobody used The Hat. I'd blast them with my wand and...

I shot up out of bed, the realization hitting.

"My goddamn wand. They blew up my wand."

Like I'd get any sleep now.

So I lay in the dark on a lumpy bed, and waited out the night. Tomorrow, before I did anything else, before I could even begin to deal with this, I had something much more important to do.

Questions and More Questions

"What you doing, Uncle Arthur?"

I looked up to find that the two sprogs, plus George and Vicky, were all gathered around watching me.

"I'm making a wand," I said, like it should have been obvious.

"Can I have one too?" asked one spawn of the diminutive devil, looking as smart as her sister in her school uniform.

"Me too," said the other demon spawn.

"Wands are only for wizards."

"And witches," added George.

"Yeah, I suppose," I grunted, then went back to my work.

"Arthur, don't go filling their heads with all this nonsense," warned Vicky, looking nervous and trying to laugh it off.

"Come on, they already know, don't they?" I asked, suddenly aware I wasn't sure if her daughters knew anything about the magical world. I'd never talked about it with them, but I guess I'd assumed Vicky had said a thing or two. But no, of course she hadn't, as before her husband met with an "accident" she'd kept this life from them all, knowing they wouldn't understand. Or he wouldn't. But things were different now, weren't they?

"Don't you think it's about time they knew?" I asked.

"Knew what?" asked Tweedledum.

"Ooh, is it a secret?" asked Tweedledee.

Vicky glared at me but then reconsidered, and a wicked smile spread across her dastardly face. "If Uncle Arthur wants to tell us a story, about how to make wands, and how he got his first one, then you'll also learn a very special secret. One," she warned, "that you are never, ever, cross your heart and hope to die, to tell anyone else. This is between us only. Promise."

"We promise," the girls chorused.

I did my own glaring, as I wasn't big on talking about my past, especially to little girls with school uniforms on, their hair in pigtails, as trusting as trusting could be.

"Fine," I said, and moved from my crouching position out on the large patio with various tools strewn about where I'd been trying to get some peace and complete my work before I did anything else.

I hadn't slept, so had gone off to retrieve my tools and the wood needed to make my wand. Not normal wood, but... It's part of the story, so you'll find out soon enough. I was also still miffed as hell that I'd let my wand be destroyed. If I'd been in my right mind then it would never have happened, as wands are basically indestructible. But I'd been drained of magic, and tapped into its reserves to keep going, then being dead had negated what little power remained in the wood so it was, for a short while, as the bomb hit, just a nice stick.

"Okay," I said with a sigh brought on by a life of constant crap like this, "gather around, everyone. Pull up a chair and Uncle Arthur will tell you all about how he got to have the best wand in the whole world."

"Yippee," squealed the girls as they dragged heavy chairs across the paving and sat on the cold metal without complaint.

George and Vicky were almost as excited, a rare glimpse into the world of The Hat.

I took a seat, wondering where to start, lost in thought for a moment as everyone stared at me impatiently. Vicky knew how I became a wizard, and after sharing the tale with her I felt bad so had also told George, along with several other things about my past. It was time, she should know about my history because it was hers too. So I should start this tale right after I finished my apprenticeship.

"A long, and I mean long, time ago, I spent a year with a very special, very scary man in Africa, in the middle of the desert. He taught me how to become a wizard." I waited for the girls to give me grief, that I was being silly and making it up, but they just stared at me, rapt.

Vicky and George exchanged confused glances, clearly expecting the same reaction.

"Um, you don't seem shocked. I just said I was a wizard."

"We know that, silly," said one.

"You do?"

"Sure. How else could you do magic?" said the other.

"Fair point."

"But... but we've never talked about what Uncle Arthur does," said Vicky.

"Oh, we know all about it. Uncle Arthur is a wizard, Aunty George is a witch, and a faery, and Mummy is their helper. Like elves help Father Christmas."

"So you believe in Father Christmas?" I asked. Vicky looked out of her depth already, which I guess is the norm when dealing with young children.

"Don't be silly, he's just made up, a kids' story, but that's what Mummy's like. An elf."

"She is, isn't she? A tiny elf with a silly nose who never stops talking." I agreed.

"Mummy does like to talk," agreed a perfect miniature person, then they both laughed.

"I am not like an elf," moaned Vicky, pouting. "But how do you know about Arthur and George?"

"Because we hear you talking, silly. You're always talking about magic and portals and Sasha the faery godmother, and Cerberus, and Hounds and vampires. All kinds of stuff."

The grown-ups exchanged worried glances. Hell, we'd always been so careful, but I guess kids are good at being quiet when they want to be.

"I think we need to start watching what we say," I offered.

"I think you're right," agreed Vicky.

"And I'm not an Aunty, am I?" asked George.

"If I'm Uncle Arthur, and you're my daughter, that should make you an... What does that make you?"

"Dunno," said George.

"Aunty George," said one rather impatient looking child. "Can you get on with the story now? We have to go to school soon."

"Good idea." I held up the length of wood, about two palms long, still rough, with lots of work to do, and said, "This is the beginning of a new wand. I lost my other one when someone dropped a bomb on it, so I have to make a new one. It will take me all day, but once finished it will allow me to harness my magic, use special symbols I'll carve, called sigils, that make my magic more focused and powerful."

"It's just a stick."

"No, it's not. It's a symbol of my power. Plus, this is no ordinary wood. It's horn of unicorn."

The girls were fascinated; Vicky and George rolled their eyes. "Don't tell them fibs, Arthur," chastised Vicky.

"I'm not. Oh, sorry, I don't mean an actual unicorn. It's the name of a very special tree. One only found in the land of fae. George, Sasha should have told you all about it."

"Never heard of it. What, do tiny unicorns grow on it?"

"Do they?" asked both children at the same time.

"No, it has never flowered, never borne fruit. There are several of these trees in the land of the fae, but they are immensely rare and very well protected, and you are never, ever, allowed to cut a branch from such a tree. Now, the trees get their name because they are a single trunk in a spiral, like a unicorn's horn, with only a few branches up high. But it really looks like a horn, so that's how it got its name. Plus, it's white, as white as your shiny teeth."

"Mummy makes us clean them twice a day," said menace one with a frown.

"But when a branch falls from the tree, which is awfully rare, it loses some of its magic, some of its essence, and it turns black like this piece here. But that magic is still waiting to be released inside it, or, um, this is hard to explain, there isn't magic inside it, but it is waiting to have some from a wizard whose own magic will activate it and bring it back to life."

"That makes no sense," said Vicky.

"I know. It's hard to explain. Okay, think of it like this. This piece of wood was once magical, now it isn't. But when I turn it into a wand, make it mine, to channel magic, then it wakes up, and it is happy again."

"A happy stick," said George with a smile.

"Don't be cheeky. Yes, a happy stick. Now, where was I?"

"You were gonna have a break because this chapter has gone on long enough," said George as she stood and wandered off. She turned and said, "Just gotta pee. Don't say another word without me."

Fair enough. Chapter break it is.

Wand of a Unicorn

"That's better," said George as she returned and sat back down.

The girls giggled. Peeing is funny.

"Now, once I became a wizard, I knew there was something missing. I'd used a rudimentary wand when training, and still had one, had carved it and everything, but I didn't feel a deep connection, not like I did with my real wand, the one I just lost. In fact, it feels terrible, like losing a limb, so I have to do this, and today, or I'm gonna be real grumpy." I poked out my tongue at the girls and they tittered.

"You're always grumpy, Uncle Arthur. Or your face is, anyway."

"I wandered the deserts, I wandered the tropics, I went up rivers and into the deepest, darkest depths of remote mountains where I met many strange people, and even stranger creatures. And they all had something in common. A staff, a wand, a talisman of some sort. Something they had a true, deep affinity with. All I had was a nice looking stick to help me focus where I was pointing my magic."

"Did you meet a faery?" asked one of the girls.

"No, not then, that would come many years later. Better than that."

"What?" they both squealed.

"I met a genuine, real life gnome."

"Arthur, stop telling fibs. I warned you," scolded Vicky.

"Cross my heart and hope to die. I was touring the country, getting up to all kinds of naughty stuff, and I had a reputation by then for being a bit of a handful, and then I met a gnome. Tiny fella he was, even smaller than your mum, so you can imagine how minute he was."

"Mummy is tiny. She buys her clothes in the same shops as us."

"I know, but that's just because she's tight and doesn't like to spend money."

"Hey, why pay more when you don't have to?" asked Vicky, affronted.

"So, this gnome was sitting underneath a tree and he was crying. I was, er, kind of in hiding, just for a week or two, as some very bad men were after me, so I was sleeping rough. Er, I mean, camping out in the countryside because it was summer. Anyway, I stumbled across this gnome."

George and Vicky rolled their eyes but the girls were loving it, leaning forward in their chairs, hands cupping their faces. Nothing like an appreciative audience to keep you telling your story.

"So, I sat down, not really thinking much of it, as I'd seen so many peculiar things by now. This gnome was all sad, crying, and I just sat down and asked if he was all right. He looked up at me, tears in his eyes, and asked if I could see him."

"What did you say?" asked Vicky, getting into my tale at last.

"I said, of course I could. Everyone knew that when a gnome cried they were visible to wizards. It was the magic leaking. The gnome said it was news to him, but we got chatting. I cheered him up, told him a joke or two, and then he checked his little gnome watch and said he had to go. He was late for something."

"Why was he crying, Uncle Arthur?"

"You know, I never found out. Sometimes it's best not to ask, and I was just trying to cheer him up, not remind him of why he was upset. So, he jumped up, but when he did, he slipped, and he broke his staff in half. He asked me if I wanted it. And I said, feeling a bit affronted actually, why would I want a broken stick? He explained that it was a rare branch from a horn of unicorn tree, that it had special powers and that my wand was rubbish, so I should carve a new one out of this rarest of woods, and it would work loads better. I said thank you, to be polite, but thought he just wanted to give me something for cheering him up so thought he'd make it up about the broken staff. And off he skipped."

"Wow," said one.

"That's so cool," said the other.

"I know, right? And since that day I've had my wand, but it got destroyed, so I'm using the spare piece to make another one."

"Right, that's enough stories for one day. Come on you two," said Vicky, hurrying the girls. "Time for school."

I put my arms out and got a fantastic hug from each girl, and then they were skipping off, just like the gnome, with Vicky scowling at me and shaking her head.

"That was a nice story, Dad. It cheered them up and stopped them fixating on the dangerous side of magic."

"I thought it might help. Plus I like to tell you a bit about myself. I'm trying to open up."

George stared at me for a while, then opened and closed her mouth a few times, before finally finding her words. "Um, I thought it was a story? I thought you were making it up."

"As if I'd do such a thing." I went back to whittling the wood to make my wand.

George stood and stared at me a while longer, but I just focused on my work. This had to be done.

I was never certain if the gnome was winding me up about it being from a fae tree, or if it was just a stick, but sometimes you have to believe, right? It makes the world a nicer place.

Plans

George left me to it. We'd have breakfast in an hour or so when Vicky returned after taking the girls to school, so I kept my mind empty and focused on my wand.

The rhythmic motions of scraping then sanding the wood until it was as smooth as silk were hypnotic, the best kind of therapy, and although it saddened me to think of my old wand, and my old house, I refused to be beaten down by the loss. It was just stuff. Wands and houses and furniture and possessions, transient items of no real importance. I was alive, my daughter was safe, and that was what counted.

Maybe it was all for the best. We could buy a new place, somewhere George and I chose together. A true home, as important to her as me. Yeah, Cerberus did me a favor, and although I wasn't quite in the mood to thank them for it, it wasn't so bad. Money wasn't an issue, and I could probably get a payout on the insurance, as the farm had been insured to the hilt, what with the unexpected always a possibility.

I chuckled as I pictured some world-weary insurance guy, an inspector who was more used to checking out property damage like cracked walls or broken roofs, coming to the farm and seeing the craters, me explaining that somebody had orchestrated a drone strike and there had been actual bombs. How would that work? What type of investigation would happen? Maybe I should keep quiet about that, just say the place blew up and leave them to figure it out? Yeah, probably be more sensible.

It felt odd to be thinking of mundane stuff like insurance and house buying when a fanatical secret organization dedicated to collecting magical artifacts were baying for my blood, but sometimes it's the only way to cope with the sheer madness, and this was definitely right up there with the craziest it had ever got.

I made a mental list of the things to be done this morning, then returned to my work, putting such distractions aside, focusing on what was important. And that was ensuring I was as powerful a wizard as possible so I could go to war.

That's what this was now.

War.

Perfection

Maybe an hour later, with my legs seized up from squatting, I blew on the wand and the last specks of dust flew away. I held up the length of wood no thicker than my thumb and stared at it, tipped it, revolved it, checked it from every possible angle.

You'd think making an unimpressive looking piece of branch into a wand would be a straightforward process, the result of so much work was just a short, straight stick with a slightly rounded end, after all, but it's a tough operation to perfect. And it had to be perfect. For it to function properly, be a conduit for my magic, it had to be flawless, perfectly aligned and balanced just so, to allow my will to flow without interruption, to gather energy and focus before I dealt with the baddies. I'd done a damn good job of it.

The wood was warm to the touch, smooth and comforting, and the sigils I'd carved were like brands from God. This was an upgrade, no doubt about it. With what I'd learned over the intervening years, this new wand had better, more powerful sigils, modifications to the originals I should have done long ago, but I liked the familiar, and couldn't bring myself to get rid of the old one. Wand 2.0 was a thing of true beauty and power, a genuine artifact in its own right.

Magic I'd learned, other aspects I'd perfected over decades of hardship and practice, their essence was instilled in the symbols I carved, forged not just with a blade but with my will. A complete, but pared down version of what I knew to be magic. Each mark held deep significance and immense potency, enough to make the wand an almost sentient thing.

It was almost perfect, it just needed a finishing touch. A little flourish on the tail of one sigil.

I felt the potential as I finished the last carving, felt something click as my blade nicked a tiny piece of wood and I was done. It was as though a spark of life had been ignited, making this something unique and very, very special. This wasn't just a talisman, a symbol, a way to focus, it was true power. I know it sounds silly, but at that moment I felt like a miracle had happened here, maybe because of the focus and will I used to forge it, maybe some anger and frustration too, but mostly it was because I put so much of myself into it, the essence of magic itself.

There were stories from the old timers about wands and staffs being almost equals in the far, distant past. Wizards spoke with awe and in hushed voices of the days when such items were like familiars, companions that took them to a whole other level of power. Some believed, others didn't, but I understood what they meant as I held my wand, like all my magic condensed down to its rawest nature. I'd always thought of it as only stories though, not the truth, but I felt it as I held this symbol of my wizard nature, the potential it contained.

Could they have been telling the truth? That once upon a time, in the days when magic was more vibrant and life was simpler, that wizards truly had sentient wands and staffs? I'd never known anyone who had one, the art seemingly lost, but there were the tales, and sometimes stories come from truth, other times not.

"Let's find out, shall we?" With the utmost care, never taking my eyes off the wand, or my focus wavering for even a moment, I checked it over one more time. The wood was not quite bone white, not cream either, more the color of aged bone. A warm white is the best I can do to describe it. But it made my heart sing, as the whiter it got, the more magic it would be able to channel, maybe even create.

The sigils were of a pale umber, darkened as they were etched into the wood and their potential readied, as if merely being a symbol of what I could do was enough to burn them into the wood. Where I held the wand was devoid of marks, then as we moved toward the end the sigils increased in number and complexity, until the tip was almost brown with a complex knot of marks.

I held the wand at arm's length, checked there was nobody about, then channeled my will, gently and cautiously—as you never use too much power when you're breaking in a new wand—down my arm, into my palm, and then into the wood itself.

It was like a gun going off. Freaky, spasming energy surged into the wand, burning my palm. My whole arm vibrated with the recoil of the wand being given its first taste of magic.

"You took your bloody time," came a cheery, almost childish voice.

I almost dropped the wand, but instead gripped it tighter and stared at it as I lifted it again warily, like it could explode in my hand if I wasn't careful.

My hand throbbed, almost pulsed as if I had an extra limb and the blood was surging into it for the first time, life flowing, energy circulating as though it was a part of me now.

"Well, aren't you going to say anything?" asked, er, no, it couldn't be, could it?

"Hello?" I said nervously, watching the sigils pulse from dull umber to a fiery orange as if beating to the rhythm of my heart. But it wasn't, as my heart was beating way faster.

"Wotcha, Arthur. Or should I call you The Hat?"

"Is that really you talking? The wand?"

"Who else could it be?" asked the slightly squeaky, yet somehow wise-sounding voice.

"Could be anyone," I mused. "Someone playing a trick on me, or I've lost my marbles. How the fuck are you talking?"

"Hey, watch the language. Were you raised in a gutter?"

"Damn, now a wand is telling me off."

"Then don't swear. What, you short of words or something? Forgotten all the beautiful words in this fine language. Although, I have to say, it's a bit limiting. But it'll do." The wand shifted in my hand, slid away from my grip a little then settled. Weirdly it felt better like this, as if it were the perfect spot, and I felt the connection between us intensify.

"Aah, that's better. Nothing like being comfortable to let the juices flow."

"What are you talking about? You're a piece of wood, you don't get comfortable. Or have juices. Um, and how are you talking? Are you alive?"

"Ah, the great philosophical debate that has perplexed the most sage of wizards for millennia. Just what is life, and how do we define it?"

"No idea. Just asking."

"Then I guess I am alive. I am, therefore I exist. Gotta say, it's confusing. One minute there I was, or wasn't, being nothing, and now here I am, a powerful stick. Kind of messes with your head. Er, you know what I mean."

I honestly didn't. So it was true, you really could have a sentient wand. But how, and why? Was this real? I squatted, much to the protest of my knees, but this needed serious consideration, and I wasn't sure how to handle it.

"Okay, let's start at the beginning. How are you alive? If you are."

"BY THE POWER OF GRAYSKULL!" boomed the wand, vibrating madly in my hand as white light fizzed from its tip.

"Hell!" I screamed, falling backward onto my bony ass and nearly dropping it.

"Haha, haha, so funny. You should see your face. Just messing with you, dude. What's life without laughter?"

"You almost gave me a heart attack. Haha," I laughed nervously, "you're funny. But, um, you can't see, can you?"

"Sure I can. I'm a magical wand brought to life through the power of your skill and your need, your will and determination. I can see plenty good. It's kinda confusing, as I can see in all directions, but I'm sure I'll get used to it. It's been what, five minutes? Plenty of time to get accustomed to things."

"I guess. So you can think, see, all that stuff?" I moved the wand close to my eyes and stared at it, but it hadn't grown any eyes or got a mouth or anything. "Are you talking out loud?"

"Of course I'm not talking out loud, are you mad? I'm a stick!"

"Ah, right."

"Hmm. So, we gonna do this?"

"Do what?"

"Go deal with Cerberus and those treacherous vampires. Dirty buggers, pardon my cursing, but they have to pay. Nobody messes with us. Don't they know who they're dealing with?"

I smiled at my wand, then said, "I like you. A lot. Yeah, we'll deal with them. Me and you, buddy. The Hat and, um, what's your name?"

"Name? Hadn't thought about that. Hang on a moment." The wand quieted, the sigils dulled, and it cooled a degree or two, then it vibrated, brightened, and I felt the power return. "Wand, call me Wand."

"Took you a while to come up with that, did it?"

"Don't be cheeky. You got a better name?"

I thought for a moment, going though different options, thinking of something menacing and powerful, something to frighten my enemies, a name I could call out as I ran into battle and let rip with my... "Yeah, Wand sounds pretty good. Okay, Wand, what now?"

"Now? Now we make a plan." Wand squirmed and turned to "face" toward the house. "Well, hello. Who's this foxy lady?"

"That's my daughter, and don't talk about her like that. If you're some kind of pervert then you can go right back where you came from. Speak like that again and I'll snap you over my knee like the twig you were."

"Oh, sorry, I apologize. How disrespectful. Don't know what came over me. It's the power of the fae. She's faery, right?"

"Half."

"They're special, they can do funny things to a guy."

"Not this one, she's my daughter and you treat her with respect." What was I talking about? It was a piece of wood. He, it, wasn't going to treat her in any way at all.

"Hey, George," I said as she came and stood next to me, quizzical look on her face.

"So, you finished?"

"Finished?"

"The wand. Can I see?"

"Oh, right. Um, sure," I said cautiously. I held up Wand and he spun in my palm. "Show off," I muttered.

"What was that?" asked George.

"Nothing, just talking to the new wand. Us wizards do that kind of thing, they're like one of the family.

"Hey, I am family. Nice to meet you, George."

George peered closely at Wand then smiled and said to me, "That's a cool trick. How'd you do it? Is it powerful? It looks it."

"It wasn't me, it was him. Honest."

George looked from me to Wand, and Wand bowed in my hand, bending my wrist until it cracked. "Pleased to meet you. Shake?"

George met my eyes and I nodded my head. She reached out, took the tip of Wand, and shook. "Nice to meet you, er?"

"Wand, the name's Wand. I came up with the name myself."

"Nice to meet you, Wand." George released her grip, turned back to me, and said, "Breakfast's ready. Vicky's back, and we have a lot to do."

"Um, okay. You don't seem very surprised. About Wand, I mean."

George studied me for the longest time, and I stood there like a lemon, Wand held at arm's length, not sure what to make of it.

"Oh, damn, you're serious? This isn't a trick, a joke?"

"No."

"Oh."

"Breakfast?" I suggested.

"And coffee," said George, watching Wand like it could attack. Hopefully, it wouldn't.

So, we wandered up to the house, me still holding Wand out in front.

I smiled. How cool is this? A sentient wand. Awesome.

Awkward Introductions

"Who's the kid?" asked Wand as we entered through the French doors into the living room.

"Quiet, that's Vicky. I know it's hard to believe, but she's an adult."

"Haha, very funny. She's tiny, like a munchkin. Where does she get her jumpers, Tiny Moms R Us?"

"Dad, stop being silly, she'll hear you," warned George, giving me the terrifying look all the women in my life had perfected long ago.

"It's not me, it's him," I protested.

George dragged on my arm and pulled me to a halt as we watched a distracted Vicky tidying away toys from the rug by the sofas. "Are you on the level about this? I don't know whether you're making this up or not."

"George, I am not making this up. The wand, er, Wand, came to life I guess, once I finished making him. It can happen, there are stories about it. About them becoming true artifacts. Now I've got one." I couldn't help grinning, this was just so damn cool. A sentient wand, what wizard could ask for more? I wondered what he knew, what he could teach me. Some of the tales were pretty wild.

"This is ridiculous. Wands can't talk."

"I can," said Wand.

"But you haven't got any lips."

"That's what I said."

"What can I tell you guys? I'm magic, pure magic."

"But... Um, ugh, this is nuts."

"Nuttier than you being a faery and able to open Paths into Faery and do all your other sparkly magic?" asked Wand.

"Fair point. How'd you know about that?" she asked, peering closely at Wand.

"Because I'm a magical wand brought to life by the power of Arthur's will and awesomeness."

"Oh, okay."

"Cool, eh? And I am pretty awesome."

"Very," agreed George, not looking completely honest about it. "How come we can hear you? Are you actually talking?"

"It's complicated. You guys can hear me because you're linked. I don't think anyone else can. Shall we try?"

And with that I felt an insistent tugging and Wand shot off toward Vicky, my hand wrapped tight around him.

"Hey, tiny, I'm Wand, wanna party?"

George sniggered and I yanked hard on Wand until he eased up on the pulling. Vicky ignored us and carried on tidying. Guess she couldn't hear.

"She's got a nice bum," said Wand, as we all watched her crawling around collecting dolls and putting them in a basket.

"Now I know he's real. You'd never say that about Vicky," said George.

"See, told you."

"Oh, hey," said Vicky, putting the last doll away then standing.

"Hey."

"Is it ready?" she asked, glancing at Wand. "Looks nice."

"Let her hold me, Arthur. Maybe suggest I get put in her back pocket."

"Shut up." I warned.

"Arthur, I was only asking." Vicky's lip trembled, and I knew what was coming. No, anything but the tears.

"Sorry, I wasn't talking to you. Um, there's been a development. My, er, my wand, well, it, he, er, he's become, er, alive."

"Oh, is that right? You were talking to your wand?" Vicky rested her hands on her hips and glared. She was good at glaring, she practiced on the kids all the time.

"Yes. Only you can't hear him, because he's magical, but he can talk and he can see." It sounded lame, but I figured best to be truthful or I'd end up in all kinds of trouble, getting all kinds of grief.

"There's no need to be mean. I just wanted to have a look."

"Honest, it's true. But you can't hear him."

"Fine, be like that. I was going to say it looked lovely, but if you're going to be silly."

"Let her hold me, trust me on this," said Wand.

"Okay, if you're sure?" I said.

"Sure about what?" asked Vicky.

"I was talking to Wand. Here, take hold, and don't say I didn't warn you." I passed Wand to Vicky, who took him with a frown, annoyed at me.

The moment she took hold and I released Wand, she froze, and I don't mean just went still and stopped talking for a bit, which was always good. I mean froze solid, not a flicker of movement.

After two minutes George and I were seriously worried, but she was still stuck in place. After five minutes I wondered if I should risk taking Wand back, but George and I discussed it and agreed to wait. What the hell was this all about?

After another five minutes I was ready to do whatever it took, but she snapped out of it with a jolt, gasped for breath, crumpled to the floor, and dropped Wand.

"A little help here"? asked Wand from the rug.

Ignoring it, him, we rushed to Vicky and got her standing. Her eyes were rolled back in her head but they slowly came down and she focused on us, her chest heaving. A smile spread across her flushed face.

"I like him," she said, then she bent, picked up Wand, and kissed the tip. Which was weird, and disturbingly arousing.

"I like her too," said Wand.

"Did you hear that?" I asked.

"No, Wand said I can only hear him if I hold him, but we're friends now. Let's have breakfast." And with that Vicky began whistling and wandered off toward the kitchen.

"What did you say to her?" I asked.

"Haha, that's for us to know. Private, mind your own business. But she knows the deal, we got to know each other. And wow, she's a werewolf. I love werewolves."

"I think I need that coffee now," I said with a sigh.

"Me too," said George.

And so it was that I had one of the weirder mornings of my life. Not the weirdest, but it came a close second.

Out On My Own

Wand had a gazillion questions about anything and everything. Seemed that although his knowledge was varied and vast, on certain topics he was clueless. He mostly knew everything I knew, which was disturbing and worrying, like a clone but without the good looks and body to die for. But there were gaps, and some things about me and my life he had no inkling of, so he asked, a lot.

Guess it was an incomplete tapping into my mind and memories. What he did know a lot about, and this would be invaluable, was magic. Being forged from magic, from faery wood—and I'll have to tell you the true story of how I got this most rare of woods some time—gave him an encyclopaedic knowledge of magic. From the fae themselves to the Nolands, to the essence of magic, he said he knew a lot and would share.

But boy did he like to talk.

What became very annoying very rapidly was his incessant chatter and inability to shut up. It was like Vicky on speed. Eating breakfast was a laborious process as every time he said something and George or I answered, Vicky butted in wanting to know what Wand had said, so everything had to be repeated. Still, at least we all got to know each other.

Part of me, a large part, still couldn't believe this was real, that I'd somehow, through my power of concentration and my advanced skill as a wizard, been able to create life itself of a very rare, and very sought after kind. Any wizard would give their right arm to own such an artifact. This went beyond books, even a Teleron, this was like having a personal assistant that could tap into an esoteric library at will and provide you with intel you could never hope to find out alone.

Plus, life gets lonely, so company is always good.

What bugged me was his accent. I couldn't quite place it, and it kept nagging at me, but I couldn't figure it out. How did a wand have an accent? It was all in my mind, a voice coming through the magical grapevine, so was this really how he sounded? Did he sound the same way to George?

After breakfast, as we sat around avoiding discussing what we needed to discuss, like my house being bombed and being set up by the vampires and Cerberus, neither of whom had been in contact, I just had to ask.

"What's the accent? I can't decide what it is."

"Accent?" asked Wand.

"Yeah, your voice. It's got a twang to it but I don't know where it's from."

"What did he say?" asked Vicky, glancing from me to Wand who was now in my left hand, seemingly more comfortable being held than stuffed in my pocket, something he'd have to get used to anyway.

"Just let me talk, then I'll tell you," I growled.

"Fine." Vicky was in a huff, but it was tough.

"Never thought about it. Although, I've only been alive for half an hour or so, maybe that's the reason. Anyway, what's your accent?"

"Mine's just, ugh, um, dunno. A general British one I guess. I traveled a lot, it gets mixed up."

"He sounds a bit Australian," said George.

"No he doesn't. He's definitely British."

"Not to me. Hey, Wand?"

"Yes?"

"Do you sound different to different people?"

"Guess so. Depends on how it comes through the ether. I could sound like anything. To me, listening to my own voice, I sound like you and Arthur. Just normal sounding."

"That's it!" I shouted. "You sound Welsh."

"No I don't."

"You do, just slightly, a little bit." I thought, but then decided I was wrong. "Or maybe west country. Or northern."

"Arthur, you're getting confused," chastised Wand, like he was talking to a little kid. "I'm whatever makes you feel most comfortable. My accent is what you find easiest to listen to."

"Oh, so definitely nothing like Vicky then." I sighed as Vicky opened her mouth to speak after hearing her name mentioned. "Later, okay?" I said, holding my hand up in front of her face.

"Dad, can we please talk about yesterday?"

"Sure, honey. Sorry, we don't need this distraction. Look, both of you, this is serious and things are going to get dicey. Very dicey. The vamps double-crossed us, meaning Ivan might be involved, and Cerberus will be gunning for me once they discover I'm alive. We have to be careful, or I do."

"Won't they come for me too?" asked Vicky, concerned not for herself but for her kids.

"No, they won't. Carmichael wants me dead for trying to take the artifacts, even though they'd already moved them, and the vampires won't be interested in you. No, this is all on me."

"You sure?" asked George.

"I am. Look, let's get this day started. George, oh light of my life, I have an important task for you. I want you to scour the estate agents, and I want you to find us the perfect home. Something with a nice large farmhouse, at least five acres, preferably flat land for horses to be, um, whatever you do with horses. Run about a bit? Canter? Is that what you do?" George rolled her eyes so I continued. "Somewhere we can build the stables and whatnot, and if you can find something close enough so we don't have to move the portal from the barn then all the better. But really, pick wherever you want, as long as it's not too far from the coast."

"You mean it? I can choose?" George's face lit up, already dreaming of her future business.

"I do."

"And it's equestrian."

"What is?"

"Things to do with horses. Not horse stuff. Equestrian. And you mean it, I can run an equestrian center. Training, stabling, whatever I want?"

"I mean it from the bottom of my heart. You find it, I'll buy it."

"How much can we spend?"

I did some quick calculations, thinking of the money I had stashed, the money in banks, and artifacts I could sell. "Just find something you like, something you will feel comfortable in, meaning nothing like Vicky's place, and we'll see."

"It is a bit big," admitted Vicky. "And I don't like having the staff around, gives me the creeps."

"So move. Ivan wanted what was best for you, but he picked somewhere he could hide too, and he put people here to watch you."

"I thought maybe he had. But the girls love the place, all the space."

"Buy something with the space outside but a smaller house."

"That's what I'm going to look for," said George.

"Good girl." I knew she'd find the perfect property, something that would suit us, feel like a home. "Well, what you waiting for?"

"You mean now?" she asked, shocked. "That feels weird. Our house just got blown up. Shouldn't we, er, wait?"

"For what? Go find something, we'll make them an offer they can't refuse, and kick some solicitor butt to get the paperwork through fast. We'll be in within a few weeks, maybe less."

"If you're sure?"

"I am."

George smiled and dashed off to get ready. In ten minutes she was out the door, said she'd do some shopping for clothes for both of us, and look for property at the estate agents down in Cornwall then maybe online after that if she found nothing.

Vicky and I were finally alone.

"You're a good father," said Vicky, reaching out and taking my hand.

"My daughter nearly got blown up last night," I said. "I'm a terrible father, the worst."

"No, you aren't. You sent her out today so she'd be away from you, right?"

"Of course! This is gonna be one hell of a day. And I want you to stay here, Vicky. No coming with me today, okay? I don't know what will happen, but it won't be good."

"Okay, Arthur, I promise." Vicky was sincere, knew this was more serious than anything we'd ever been involved in before. She had to think of the girls.

"Can I come?" asked Wand.

"You, my sticky friend, go everywhere with me."

"Nice!"

As I placed Wand down on the table and took a sip of coffee, I heard a crack as the window smashed and Vicky's eyes went wide. A red dot leaked from the center of her forehead as she slumped forward, slamming her face on the table.

I didn't need to look, but I had to. I sprang up, pulled her shoulders back, and stared at the bullet wound in her head. I laid her head gently on the table as my tears fell.

Someone had just assassinated Vicky.

This Will Hurt

My world came crashing down in a spectacular way. Every job we went on I was amazed she didn't get herself killed. She was fearless, gung-ho, and always up for it, just like me I guess, and simply didn't have the skills to cope with the gangster life, but she'd always come through relatively unscathed. I expected her to die, but also somehow always believed she wouldn't. She had kids she adored, was always frisky like a puppy, and cute in her own annoying miniature way, and I couldn't truly picture her as being dead.

But she was.

My heart stuttered, my body lost all control, and I found it hard to breathe. This couldn't be happening, no, no, no. Not Vicky. She had children, they'd be alone. She had so many years ahead of her, and she'd be cursing from beyond the veil that she never got to see them grow up to be rulers of the universe and the snub-nosed, much smarter than everyone else, blond gods they were destined to be.

Tears fell, and I couldn't stop them even though there was a gunman somewhere outside. Had they just come for Vicky? I bet they had. Who? Cerberus? The vampires? Someone else?

With blood oozing from the wound, Vicky's head sideways on the table, dead, vacant eyes staring at me, accusing me, I realized for the first time just how much she meant to me. I loved her, truly I did. She'd insinuated herself into my life, my very being, and I couldn't imagine it without her.

"No, I will not accept this," I said, determined. I looked into those dead eyes and I nodded. "I'm coming to get you."

I leapt up, grabbed the bread knife from beside the hacked loaf, and without pausing or thinking about what I was doing, I plunged it straight through my chest, between my ribs, and into my heart.

"I'm gonna regret this," I croaked, before I croaked it.

It really, and I mean really, hurt.

You Die, I Die, We All Die

"Fucking hell, that really hurt. You should sharpen your knives. It felt like stabbing a blunt stick through my heart," I said to Vicky.

"Huh?" Vicky, looking even smaller than usual, dragged her eyes away from the, I guess intimidating to some, towering figure before her and slowly focused on me. "Arthur? What did you say?"

"I said your bread knife needs sharpening. I just stabbed myself with it and it fucking killed. Haha."

"Are we dead? Am I dead? And, er, you what? You killed yourself? Why?"

"To come get you, of course," I said like it was obvious. It was to me, anyway.

"Blimey, bit sinister here, isn't it?" said Wand, who I realized I was clutching in my left hand.

"You get used to it," I grumbled. "Hi." I waved at Death, who was standing motionless, looking awesome as usual. Full black robe, face in shadow, huge fucking scythe, wind blowing the tattered cloth in a suitably menacing way, blah, blah, blah.

"Hell, Arthur. This is, ah, unexpected."

"Good, because I don't plan on staying. Um, hang on, you mean you weren't expecting me?" I knew my name had multiple entries in his ledger, heck, I'd been here often enough, and he always knew I was coming.

"That's what I said. It's one guest at a time, those are the rules."

"You know me, a maverick."

"You know each other!" Vicky shrieked, unable to stop staring at Death.

He stood several feet away from us, the water of the mist-drenched lake lapping at his feet, or I assume there were feet under the cloak. The pebble beach was infinite, the sky was dark and threatening, but it was pretty boring once you got over the shock.

"Yeah. Imaginary Figure of Death, this is Vicky. Vicky, this is—"

"Death," boomed Death. "And I am not imaginary, I am real. Real in the sense that this is how you can deal with dying and passing on."

"On? Where to?" asked Vicky, tugging at her ponytail, looking panicked.

Death shrugged. "To wherever you deserve to go."

"So there is an afterlife? You really are Death?"

"I told you I'd met him," I said, put out that she'd obviously never believed me.

"But I didn't think you meant, um, really met him, like in the flesh."

"There is no flesh, only bone," said Death.

"Okay, we get it," I said, "No need to try to be dramatic. Right, let's get down to business." I knew these things were best done sooner rather than later. Bodies can decompose, dogs get hungry, birds can peck out eyes, all that good stuff. The sooner we got back, the better. I jut hoped I hadn't made one colossal screw up with this, otherwise I'd just ruined a good shirt and an even better body. It was the only one I had, too. Shirt and body.

"You have no business here," said Death. He waved a hand and his desk and chair appeared. The ledger fell from nowhere and landed with a boom on the desk as he walked over and sat. He jabbed his infinite scythe into the pebbles so it didn't topple over, then arranged his cloak.

"Yet here I am." I got a bad feeling as I took Vicky's arm and slowly walked her over to Death. She was dazed, understandably confused, and scared as hell. "Don't worry," I whispered, "I have a plan."

"A cunning one?" she asked, full of hope.

"You bet." I winked.

We stood either side of Death. Vicky swayed, looking pale and generally terrible, nervous as hell, which I got, and I tried to hold back the rising tide of panic as I contemplated being out of lives and having no chance of doing what I'd planned. Or if I could do it no matter how many lives I had left. Was this the worst idea I'd ever had? I'd made some very dubious decisions in my time, but this could be the winner.

Death flipped through the pages, found the right one, ran a bony finger down line after line, then paused.

"Here we are. Vicky. Yes, you're here. Gunshot to the head, eh? Nasty."

Vicky put a hand to her forehead but the wound wasn't there. "Is that how I died? Someone shot me?"

"Right through the forehead," I offered, which probably wasn't a good idea. She fainted. I left her there, this would be easier without her.

"What's that asterisk?" I asked, peering over Death's hunched shoulder and squinting at the spidery writing.

"Oi, no peeking. I've warned you about this."

"But what is it?"

"Hmm, this is most unusual. Wait, let me check." Death flicked through to the back of the mighty tome and covered the pages with his arm so I couldn't see, like we were kids taking an exam. He muttered to himself and then moved to where I recalled my entries were. He searched for my name, then muttered again, slammed the book closed, and it whooshed up into the dark sky and was gone.

"I knew it. You aren't in, not for this, so it never happened."

"But it did. It has. I just ran a bloody bread knife through my heart."

"Yes, but it's not in the book. You weren't meant to do it."

"But I did," I protested.

Death shrugged his shoulders, pushed away from the desk, and stood. It all vanished, leaving him standing ten feet away holding his scythe. Wind blew his tattered cloak, but there was no wind.

"What happens now?" I asked. "What was the asterisk?"

"It's for when things don't go according to plan. It means something different will happen, something out of the ordinary."

"And this is ordinary?"

"Is to me. And everyone else. Everyone dies, then they meet me, or one of my like."

"I want to swap," I blurted, panicking about time now. "I want to swap one of my remaining lives, heck, all of them, I don't care, I want to trade for Vicky returning."

"Can't, she's dead."

"Bollocks. I've died loads of times, and returned, so why can't she?"

"Because she has no extra lives. You shouldn't either. It's not how it works. Fae have no place interfering, I've warned them about that." Death sounded genuinely put out, which I guess you would if someone interfered with a business you'd run smoothly since the beginning of time.

"But I have, and I want to swap. Send her back, let her live, and take my extra lives. She had the asterisk, that means there's a chance, that hers isn't a final death. And if I'm not meant to be here, that means this life didn't count." I thought about that, what it meant, then realized I was right. "Aha, it's already happened. I'm not registered to die now, but I have, so that means this death didn't count for me, so it must have counted for Vicky. Right, right?"

"Maybe," mumbled Death.

"So we have a deal?"

"No. It's most irregular. I won't stand for it."

"But you have to," I whined. "I can't let Vicky die, I love her. She's my friend."

"Everyone dies," said Death, not really bothered.

"Not Vicky, and not me. Not now. Come on, you can do this, and you know you can. It's up to you. Plus the book wouldn't lie. You have to send me back, as I'm not dead, and Vicky comes with me. I came to get her, to swap. If my death doesn't count neither does hers."

"Fine, fine," he said, exasperated. "You get to trade, just this once. But be warned, Arthur Salzman, this exchange means there will be an entry for this death of yours. And it could be your last."

"That's what you always say."

"One day, I'll be right."

"Haha, so this isn't the final death?" I said, catching him out on the slip.

"Just fuck off." Death waved his hand, the world went wobbly, pain hit like a slap in the face with a spiked wet tea towel, and I grabbed Vicky hurriedly, wrapped my arms around her, and we both split apart into nothingness.

I don't know what's worse, dying, or having to face life again. Both are pretty shit to be honest.

A Realization

I exploded back to life with a painful gasp followed by a grunt, and maybe a high-pitched scream. For several seconds I didn't know who or where I was, and panic flooded my system as hormones, as shocked as I was about the whole life thing, flushed through my brain, leaving me terrified and aware of how fragile I was. A deep dread of being alone filled me, and I curled up in a ball, legs tucked up, arms wrapped around them, and I cried.

I felt horrible. Nobody loved me, nobody cared, I was useless and I wasn't even a human being, not really. Just lumps of flesh held together by pointlessness. The Hat was absolutely freaked out.

Then reality hit with a vengeance. Everything came flooding back and I shook away the waking nightmare and poked a hand through my shirt. The hole was clean, my skin unblemished, just hairy, and I scowled as I noted the gray. The knife lay beside me on the floor.

Scrambling to my feet in a panic of concern, I grabbed hold of the chair as my legs buckled. Vicky still sat motionless, head against the table, but there was no pool of blood, no sign that she'd bled out. She could have just been sleeping like we both had on many an occasion when exhaustion took over.

By now my heart was beating so fast I half-expected to be meeting Death yet again after it exploded in my chest, but it was merely a combination of worry about Vicky and recuperating after being punctured. I stepped aside, hoping this had worked, unsure if it had, if what happened was real.

All I could think of was Vicky and how my life wouldn't be the same without her. It would be empty, and colder, and okay, a lot quieter, but boy would I miss her. It was a strange feeling, as Vicky annoyed the hell out of me on a scale I'd never imagined possible before we met, but she was also like a ray of perky, always frisky sunshine in my life. Brightening my day even as she addled my brain with her incessant chatter.

She couldn't be dead. I wouldn't allow it.

Gently, I took hold of her head and lifted it off the table, wincing as I expected it to be stuck fast. I couldn't look as I eased her back in the chair until she was sitting slumped with her head lolling back a little.

Then I looked.

There was no bullet hole, there was just a red mark where her head had hit the table and had been pressed for what could have been several seconds or several hours. I checked my watch. Yep, several seconds was all this had taken.

I checked her neck but there was no pulse, and as the seconds ticked by with excruciating slowness I wondered if something had gone wrong.

Then her eyelids fluttered and sprang open, eyes wild, darting left to right. She choked as she took in a huge lungful of air, coughing and spluttering as she banged on her chest like a trainee paramedic who should consider a different career path.

"Easy, just breathe. Focus on your breathing, nothing else."

Vicky turned to me and focused her eyes as fear took hold and she turned bright red. She nodded, eyes panicked, and her chest rose as she tried to suck down air. It was touch and go for a while, but finally she got it under control. Up, down, up, down, rhythmic breathing, me doing the same, her copying what I was doing. We were in sync and soon her color returned to normal. She put a hand to her head, feeling around for the bullet hole, then lowered it and checked her fingers, shocked, frowning as she stared at me, questioning.

"You saved me," she croaked. "You could have died, permanently. You risked everything for me."

"I love you," I said, meaning it like I'd never meant it before. And then, I bent and kissed her, right on the lips, with a sensitivity and passion that surprised me and concerned me deeply. It felt right, it felt normal, and we didn't flinch or break apart in shock or say anything stupid. We lingered, savoring the warmth of each other's lips, feeling the energy, the tension and emotion, the closeness, the way we were connected. As my stomach fluttered, I understood I had deep feelings for this mini-menace from the burbs.

Finally, we broke apart, and she whispered, "I love you too."

Hurriedly, I said, "Here, let me check you over." I made sure she was okay and wasn't hurt from cracking her head, but she seemed fine. Her pulse steadied, although it was a little fast, and she insisted on getting up.

We stood there, facing each other for an awkward moment, then I said, "Sorry about that. The kiss. I was just so relieved you're okay."

Vicky touched her lips as if as confused as me about how it felt. "It's okay, I understand. Arthur, you saved me, you risked so much. Why?"

"Because we're a team, and I'd do anything to protect you. Plus, you'd only haunt me and give me grief, and I'd rather you annoy me in person than from beyond the veil."

Vicky smiled, but she knew as well as I did that my words were a defense-mechanism to cover up something we'd both only realized at that moment. We loved each other. Was it a sexy times, lick your bottom, love? Or a deep friendship where the lines get blurred merely because one is male, the other female? We didn't know, and that's confusing. There had been other times over the years when we'd got into awkward situations and passion had flared, but nothing like this, not as deep and powerful.

"I would, you know? I'd haunt you and talk about the girls and never give you any peace."

"Just like now you mean?"

And with that the spell was broken. We were back being Arthur and Vicky, ace wizard and annoying sidekick.

"What if that had been your final life?"

I shrugged, "If it was my time then it was my time. I'm not scared of dying, just of how you guys would cope with me gone."

"It was very brave, and I owe you everything." Vicky was serious, and I understood, didn't try to brush it off as that would cheapen her gratitude, which wouldn't be right.

"My pleasure. I told you, back last year, that I'd look after you. I don't break promises, ever. I look after those I care about, if I possibly can, even if they get into trouble because they know me."

"It's the life we all chose."

"I know, but it doesn't make it hurt any less. Let's have a coffee, I really need one."

So we made coffee, and we sat at the table, stunned, letting our fragile minds process our resurrection. We avoided the subject of the kiss, like all sensible adults would when confronted with something that should be discussed immediately.

Time for Revenge

I checked out the house and grounds but the gunman was long gone. The staff had seen nothing, which was dodgy as fuck as I knew full well they weren't real gardeners or maintenance guys. They were Ivan's men, here to protect Vicky. Piss poor job of it they'd done.

Sure there'd be no more attempts on Vicky's life, and getting concerned about my own safety, I called George and told her a version of the story, that someone had tried to kill Vicky. She promised to remain vigilant and then I arranged to meet her back at Vicky's in the evening. Would they go after George? I hadn't thought they'd be after Vicky, but maybe because of her tech skills they wanted her gone in case she tried to take revenge. What about everyone else involved? I called around, everyone was fine, so I warned them, but that was about all I could do.

By then it was late morning, I got together a few basics, told Vicky to be careful, and headed out the door.

I drove back into the city, unsure what to do. Everyone had gone quiet, meaning Ivan. No way he wouldn't have been all over this, asking where the goodies were, or calling to give me a bollocking for screwing up.

As if on cue my phone rang, so I pulled over and took the call.

"You set me up."

"Arthur, it's not like that, I promise." Ivan sounded stressed, and he was usually as emotional as a meditating stick. He kept his emotions in check, so much so I often wondered if he'd been emptied of such things by his past degradations. He sounded tired too. The daytime was probably a struggle but I didn't care.

"No," I snapped, "what is it like then? You set me up, all of us, your own sister, man, to raid Cerberus when all the while you'd been watching, waiting for Cerberus to move the goodies so you could go get it while they thought they'd pulled a fast one on us."

My words were rapid-fire, full of scorn. I wanted to reach down the phone and throttle him. Maybe there was an app?

"You tipped off Cerberus, told them the plan, somehow got them to believe it, so you could have me go through this shit. Expendable, right? Just a way for you lot to get Mikalus' damn books."

"I didn't know."

There was silence, he said nothing more, and I didn't speak, just tried to figure out if I could trust him. He'd always been on the level, but he was a powerful man, and he was a vampire, and he had a very scary boss.

"You're a liar. You got us into this, you made me do this, and you knew. You knew it was a fool's errand. Well, guess what, someone just came to Vicky's, and your people there did nothing. She got shot, by a fucking sniper, right through the goddamn brain." Let him think on that for a moment.

"Oh, and if that isn't enough, someone, and we can all guess who, dropped a fucking bomb on my farm last night. I was with George, she could have been killed. You screwed us royally. Did you even think this through? What's wrong with you?"

"She's... she's dead?"

I hung up on him.

Bad News

An hour later I was sitting in the park by the boating lake when Ivan called back. I was surprised it had taken him so long to find out what really happened. Part of me wanted to believe he was a pawn in all this like the rest of us, but I suspected I would be disappointed.

"You could have told me she wasn't dead."

"Why should I? You lot didn't care about us when you got us involved in this. I assumed you'd have expected her to get killed once this was over. We had nothing to bargain with once we got screwed, so obviously Cerberus would want revenge on us. Probably thought we were part of the whole plan."

"So Vicky's okay?"

"Yeah, she's fine."

"You told me she got shot in the head," said Ivan, confused.

"She did. I traded in, her life for mine."

There was a long pause while he figured that one out. "You traded in a life? For my sister? It could have been your last."

"I know, man, but it's Vicky. I care about her, even if you don't."

"I... I don't know what to say. This evens the score, no more favors owed. I'll never ask again."

"You don't get it, do you? Even if you did ask, I'd say no. You set us up, that makes us more than equal. In fact," I added, "this is far from done. Nobody messes with me and mine like this. Nobody. Not Cerberus, not you, not Mikalus. Nobody."

Ivan knew what I meant, knew my character and how precious family and friends were to me. I'd thought he was a man of honor too, obeyed the Code. "You don't touch family, Ivan. Ever."

"I know, and I never would. Mikalus, he is different."

"So what are you saying?"

"That I just spoke to people, to Mikalus himself, and you are right. It was a set-up. I honestly didn't know, he didn't tell me. I figured you'd failed, that Cerberus found out somehow. That's why I didn't call. We knew you came out empty-handed and that they must have moved everything. Mikalus has what he wanted, his precious books. He used other people, our people, to recover what he feels is his."

"And you were in the dark about it? What, he just told you because you asked?"

"Actually, yes. I asked, he told me. He seemed surprised I was shocked. Said it had to be that way so I could talk to you without looking guilty."

Ivan sounded truly annoyed, but more than that he sounded disappointed. "So they screwed you over too? Made you betray me and your own sister."

"Yes. And not they, Mikalus. He made me betray a friend, and my sister. I think of you as a friend, and this is unforgivable. I got a name. How this all happened. You won't like it."

"Tell me," I said, knowing my day would get a whole lot worse before it got better. Just when things were going well for me, this happens. I had a relationship with Candy that was going great, George was happy, Vicky was, well, Vicky, but her girls were safe, and I even slept the other night after the sexy times. I was looking forward to more of that, and I had a date tonight. Guess I'd have to cancel. No way would this resolve itself by then.

"Arthur?" Did you hear what I said?"

"Sorry, no, I was miles away." I watched an old couple walking hand in hand around the boating lake, smiling and talking to each other like they were on a first date. Maybe one day Candy and I would be like that.

"Candy," said Ivan.

Distracted, I asked, "What about her? Is she in danger?"

"You aren't listening to me. Candy, it was her."

My mind wasn't taking this in so I focused, and asked again. "What about Candy?"

"She has been playing you. I don't know for how long, but Mikalus has something on her, used her to get to you. She told him what you were doing, maybe bugged your home or something, I don't know. But she told him when you were acting, so he knew when the books would be vulnerable. I'm sorry."

"No, that can't be right. She wouldn't. We were, we... the other night we..."

"I'm sorry. I'll be in touch when I find out more. But I swear to you, I had no idea about any of this. I'll find out the truth, all of it, and they'll pay. This isn't over." Ivan hung up. I hung my head.

Life. It's really got it in for me.

Goodbye to Love

This had to start somewhere, so it started with me crying like a baby ripped from its mother's breast in the middle of the night. Dragged from feeling warm, safe, and comforted, protected, loved, and at peace, with a whole future ahead, and plunged into a nightmare of loneliness, rejection, and mockery.

I was being laughed at. This old man had believed that a beautiful young woman could have an interest in him. I thought she liked me, wanted me, found me good company. I was an idiot. She'd used me, played me for a fool, and I was sad and shamed by the whole thing.

So I sat on a bench and watched an elderly couple in love feed the ducks as I cried for my own pathetic needs and desires. I knew it was too good to be true, that I could have some peace and happiness in my life. Something for me, something to chase away the night terrors, allowing me to finally sleep through the night knowing somebody wanted to be there with me, be by my side.

Once the tears had finished falling, I dried my eyes and sat there for a while longer, trying not to think but thinking dark thoughts anyway.

"Are you okay?" asked a kind voice.

I looked up to see the man standing close to me, peering down at me with concern. His wife was several paces away, watching but not in a mean, nosy way, just concerned but knowing the two of them might be too much.

"That obvious is it?"

"You looked so sad. We were worried."

"Thank you, but I'm all right. I'll get through it, I always do."

"But it's tough, isn't it?"

"It is," I admitted.

"But you're alive?"

"Yeah."

"Then there's always another chance. That lady over there," he said as he turned and pointed at the woman, who smiled and waved back. We both waved at her in return.

"Seems nice," I said.

"She is. The best. We met three years ago today at this very place. We were both feeding the ducks, both alone. Now we come together."

"That's nice."

"So there's always tomorrow. Well, be seeing you. Sorry if I intruded."

"You didn't. And thanks, I needed that."

He nodded and walked away, took the woman's hand and they carried on their slow walk around the lake.

"That was nice of him," came a voice in my head.

I jumped a mile, taking a moment to figure out who it was. "Damn, I forgot all about you."

"Didn't want to intrude. Thought it best to leave you to deal with, er, Death, and Vicky and everything."

"Right. So, you know what's going on?"

"Sure I do," said Wand, sounding more chipper than I'd have liked.

"And?"

"And? What do you mean, and?"

"I mean, what should I do now?"

"Now you go and kill the bitch."

"That's what I was thinking."

"I know."

Some Lists are Short

If I'd made a list of everyone I had to deal with it would have gone like this.

Carmichael.

Mikalus.

Now it had a new name, and God help me, I would not be stopped.

I stood across the street from Candy's coffee shop, watched as customers came and went after the lunchtime rush. When all was quiet I took a deep breath, set my face to extra grim, not that it needed much adjusting, and strode across the road.

I pushed open the door, scowled at the bell, and then closed it behind me. After I'd checked to make sure there were no citizens inside, I turned the sign over to closed, pulled out Wand, and forced my will down into the sentient wood. It felt different to before, as if I hardly had to do a thing, and as sigils flared, a spark of joy leapt into my heart as Wand pulsed and the lock fused into the door frame, sealing us all in.

"Stay out of this," I warned Steve, who was sitting drinking a coffee by the window. Then, my heart smacking against my ribcage, depression threatening to send me screaming into the darkest recesses of my damaged mind, I marched to the back where Candy was stacking cups and plates.

Candy looked up as I approached, her smile for customers plastered on her face even though she looked dog-tired and stressed. Her face dropped when she saw me.

"Guess who?" I said, and I had to use every ounce of restraint in my body to not grab her beautiful hair and slam her face into the counter, breaking her nose and smashing her teeth.

"Arthur?" she said, trying to hide the shock. "How did it go?"

"Better than you expected, worse than I did."

We stared at each other for the longest time, her knowing I knew, but not how much, then she blurted, "I can explain."

"I'm sure you can. But in my world there is nothing you can say that will get you out of this. You do not involve my fucking kid in this shit. There are rules!" I was shouting, and Steve rushed over and put an arm on my shoulder. "What?" I snapped.

"Whoa, mate, what's got into you? You two having a barney? You need to cool it."

"Cool it? Cool it?" I snarled. "She betrayed me. She was working for the fucking vampires. She betrayed you too. She set us up, helped them. They had this all planned out, isn't that right, Candy? We were the decoys, left to get killed or whatever. Cerberus blew up my fucking house with a fucking bomb. They shot Vicky through the fucking head. My daughter was with me, a bomb landed on our house. Candy and the vampires have been playing us. And she," I jabbed a finger out to the shocked Candy, who hadn't moved a muscle, "told them exactly what we were doing and when we were going. What else did you do, Candy? How else did you betray us?"

"Mate, she wouldn't do that. You got it wrong. She's one of us. I've known her for years. Candy?"

We turned to her. She hung her head and shook gently.

"Answer him. What did you do? How deep does this go? What, you thought you'd take advantage of a stupid man who thought you liked him? I invited you to my house, I treated you with respect, wanted you in my life, my family. You betrayed me, George, you betrayed Steve, and all your own kind."

"I'm sorry," she said.

I nearly went ballistic, but I held myself in check. "Sorry!? Why, why did you do this? I liked you, I feel so stupid. That I can live with, but you must have known what Cerberus would do if we came up empty handed. You knew and you spied on me, told the vampires. You're a traitor."

"It wasn't like that, it wasn't like that at all."

"You fucking bitch," said Steve, quietly and deadly.

I'd never heard him like that, never seen him so angry, and I knew what was coming.

"No, don't change. I want to hear this before she dies."

"I'll tear you to fucking shreds. I'll eat your goddamn corpse. You know the rules. No family, no betraying your pack, no acting like a fucking traitorous bitch."

"Steve, wait," I shouted, and only just in time. His body was already cracking and he'd have been lost to the shift within seconds. But he turned to me, face red and angry, and said, "Why should I wait? She's admitted it. She's scum."

"I want to know. I need to know. We need to know what the vampires have been planning, how this worked. Because this isn't over."

"Talk," ordered Steve.

"I... I had to. Mikalus sent someone to see me. But this was after we were together, Arthur. I do like you, I really do. More than anyone I've ever met. But they sent someone, and they made me an offer. I'm sorry."

"An offer to betray me, and your own? What offer?"

"It doesn't matter. I agreed. I did as they asked. I didn't know what they were up to, I swear. They just wanted information about you, a little about Vicky, then when you got given the job, they wanted me to listen in, so they could do something while you were attacking Cerberus. But I swear, I never imagined it would come to this. I didn't know it was to put you all in danger like this. I went along with it, gave them what they wanted, but I didn't know why."

"What did you do? You bugged us?"

"You. I put it on your jacket. A small thing, so they could listen. They could be listening now. Where's your jacket?"

"It got fried when Cerberus dropped a fucking bomb on my house," I shouted, close to going off the rails again.

"I didn't know."

"That's why you stayed over, why you slept with me? To bug me. You're a whore."

Candy recoiled at the insult and I felt the worst kind of man for calling her that. I still do. But was she? Was that what she was?

"I wanted to anyway. But they said I had to do it soon, as whatever they had planned was about to happen, so I did it, I slept with you because I wanted to but because they wanted you bugged. I felt so happy that we were together, that you took me into your family, but then, in the morning, it all came back to me, what I was doing, but I did it anyway. I did it, I bugged you."

"Christ, that's low," muttered Steve.

"I hurt so much I want to throw up," I said. "You know how hard this all was for me, how much it meant. But you did it anyway. What kind of person are you?"

"I was desperate. I got caught up in it then I didn't know what to do, how to get out of it. I wanted to tell you, warn you, but I couldn't. It was too late. I was so deep into it, I panicked, thought maybe things would turn out okay. I knew they were using you, but I didn't know you were being set up. I swear."

"So you just bugged me thinking the vamps wanted to keep tabs on me? Even though it was when we had this job for them? You didn't suspect?"

"Maybe, maybe not. I don't know. I didn't want to think about it. I knew something was wrong, that this wasn't right, but I didn't know their plans."

"You sat at my table and laughed and joked with my daughter and Vicky while you planned to betray me." I couldn't imagine ever doing such a thing, to act that way. She'd seemed so relaxed, so happy, so comfortable there. How could she be like this?

"I know."

"What did they offer you?"

"Freedom. Mikalus said he could take this away, this shifting. He promised me that if they got the books, he could use one to reverse it. I'd be normal. I could have been a normal woman. I thought maybe if that happened, we could be together. I could forget this ever happened, and I wouldn't have to live like this. You saw what happened the other night. I killed those men. Things like this always happen. We get involved in wars and fights with other Wild Ones. I don't want this life, I want to be normal."

"What guys?" asked Steve.

"The ones trying to take over. I dealt with some of them. And I hate it, all this fighting. And it hurts, it hurts so much. I was offered a way out, and I took it."

"Was it worth it?" I asked with regret, with sadness, for this life is hard and I understood, I really did, but she'd still done what she did.

"No." Candy shook her head then met my gaze, and for the last time she said, "I'm sorry."

Wand was in my hand, but I didn't know how he'd react, so I switched him to my left, and as Candy stood there, and Steve tried to come to terms with it all, I punched out and smashed her throat to jelly.

She could have fought, maybe even dodged, but she didn't.

Candy thudded to the floor, twitching, and I pocketed Wand and pulled out my phone. I dialed a number.

"Cleaner."

"Candy's coffee shop, you know it?"

"Yes."

"Can you deal with a body?"

"I'm the Cleaner."

"Get it done please."

"Who is it?"

"Just another body. Do what you want with it after, but get it gone."

I hung up.

Candy stopped twitching eventually, but it took a long time.

Crushing Realizations

"I can't believe she betrayed us," said Steve, leaning over the counter to stare at Candy.

"Neither can I." I didn't know what else to say. I didn't feel like saying anything at all. If I allowed myself to think, I'd spiral down, hard. The first woman I'd felt a true connection with since George's mum and I'd just punched her in the throat and killed her. I was a bad person, I didn't deserve love, affection. I was a monster. No matter what she'd done, I shouldn't have killed her. It took something away from me, what little humanity I had left, and pushed me closer to the edge, into territory I'd always tried to avoid in my own way.

Cold. Ruthless. Uncaring.

It hurt so bad though, no matter how much I tried to suppress my emotions. She was my girlfriend. We'd laughed and joked, had some great times. She was beautiful and I thought she'd genuinely liked me. Maybe she had, maybe a little at first, but she'd stayed with me, slept with me, to get information to help the vampires. Those double-crossing bastards. Mikalus had shafted us all, and I would deal with him same as I would Carmichael.

"I have to go," I said to Steve. "You too. Don't hang around here. The Cleaner will sort this mess out, it's best if we aren't here when she arrives."

"Okay, mate. Damn," he shook his head, "I can't believe she fucked us over like this. And you, how could she do that? She liked you, you know?"

"Funny way of showing it."

"Mate, she thought you were hot, was always talking about you. She liked you, Arthur, don't go thinking that was pretense. Sure, she took it too far, got involved with the vampires, but I'm sure that was only right at the end. Until then you had a good thing going on. Damn." He leaned over the counter and took a final look at Candy, shook his head once again, then turned and gave me a hard stare.

"I know how this goes, how rotten you feel, but don't let it get to you. People are complicated, and I know I'm not the smartest, not much into deep thinking and trying to figure out the mysteries of the universe and all that, but you heard her. She liked you, she took a chance, didn't know what she was getting involved in. She screwed up, and she had to pay the price, she knew that, understood, but don't forget that this life, this shit, it's hard. Candy had her own demons to fight. She made a bad choice, now it's over." Steve slapped me on the back then reconsidered and gave me a hug.

I hugged him back, clung to him hard, and we stayed like that for a while until I could stand it no longer. If I didn't get away I was gonna crumble, so I said, "Thanks, you're a good friend. I'm sorry about Candy, I know you two had a long friendship. It must be hard for you too."

"It breaks my heart, mate, hurts so bad I can't believe it. Bloody hell, this was Candy. She was always hardcore, always tough, but she had a soft side too, you know? She was vulnerable, like the rest of us."

"I know."

With that I grunted a goodbye and left.

I walked the streets in a daze, unable to connect with what had happened, as if it had been someone else, that I was merely an observer to this. It was the only way I could cope.

I was so tired, more tired than I think I'd ever been in my life. It wasn't just lack of sleep, it was everything.

My life was crumbling around me. Everything I held dear, everything that grounded me and made me a worthwhile person was being taken away from me. In a single night my world had been turned on its head, my reality stripped away leaving a rotten core.

I deserved no better. Look what I was capable of. Look what I did when things went bad. I lashed out, I murdered, and then I felt sorry for myself afterward. Maybe I deserved all this. But maybe I didn't. Maybe I was trying to make a go of things, build myself a future, and now it was gone. No home, no girlfriend. No hope.

Only one thing remained.

Revenge.

Back to Work

At a loss what to do, I walked and I walked some more, pushing through the crowds of shoppers, out into the vast expanses of warehouses and commercial properties clinging to life on the outskirts of the city, down to the canals and the encroaching marshlands, under the flyovers and through the shanty towns and into places no citizens dared tread.

I spoke to nobody, acknowledged no familiar faces, just walked with a hard stare and a permanent scowl on my face. Leave me alone, don't come near me. The Hat is not a happy camper.

How was I going to resolve this? How was I going to finally end all this bullshit? I didn't think I could. Cerberus was a huge organization, and they had their own agenda. They'd always been around, always been a part of the magical underworld, and it created a balance. We wanted the artifacts, they wanted to hide them. It kept everyone on their toes, and maybe in a warped kind of way it was for the best. It made them even more special, treated with the appropriate respect, and nobody took ownership lightly. Sure, it would be better if Cerberus didn't exist at all, but if I killed Carmichael it would only mean another replacement and more of the same old crap.

But he'd dropped a bomb on my house. Or had he? Did he give such orders, or had it come from the very top? Carmichael had a boss, and maybe, or probably, the boss, this mysterious "He," would have to give the go-ahead for such extreme action. All I knew was they'd gone too far and had to be stopped somehow. But I was one man, and even if I managed to get myself an army, which I couldn't, then we'd be small-fry compared to them. The Hounds were fierce, fanatical, dangerous, well-trained, and well-armed too. Even a horde of wizards would have a hard time destroying them, and this was but one tiny faction of the organization as a whole.

Sure, Cerberus was based here in the UK, but there were other groups spread throughout the country, and countless more worldwide. Removing Carmichael would do nothing, same as getting rid of his predecessor had done nothing but eventually make all this come to pass.

But no way could I let this go, not a chance.

And what about the vampires? Was Ivan on the level? I needed to see him, look into his eyes and give him the opportunity to explain. If I thought for a moment he was lying, that he put me and Vicky in true danger, knowing the likely outcome, then I'd kill him, no matter that he was Vicky's brother. Then there was Mikalus.

He was the vampire head, the leader they'd been craving for centuries. Powerful, immortal, sort of, and obviously without much in the way of a moral compass.

What a mess.

By the time the afternoon had come and gone, the sweltering sun had burned away my tears but not my aching heart, leaving a focus born of desperation and depression.

I made my way back to my car, formulating a rudimentary plan as I went, then I drove to Vicky's. I may have been a broken man, but I wasn't dead yet, so I'd do what I always did.

Keep on coping and hope that one day things would get better.

A House Full

"Motherfucker," I growled. Wand was out of my pocket, screaming "Yippee," as the sigils flared and my will shunted down hard and furious. Wand was raring to go, as it seemed his newfound sentience had him craving release, and the pressure built until I suspected he would do a fine job even without me.

I stormed across the kitchen, ready to blast Ivan into the afterlife, but Vicky stepped away from the large island and rushed to intercept. George stayed seated at the table, looking shell-shocked and nervous.

"Arthur, please, wait. Hear what he has to say."

I moved Vicky aside gently, not letting my anger be directed at her, but stepped right up to Ivan. "You betrayed us. You were part of this, you had to be."

Ivan put up his hands and said, "I swear to you, I wasn't. As I said on the phone, and I was telling the truth, I had absolutely nothing to do with this. I spoke more with Mikalus, just to get some things straight, and he has the books, and more besides. Cerberus attacked you, Candy bugged you so Mikalus would know exactly when to strike. You were expendable to him, all of you were. I'm sorry. I'm ashamed to be a part of this. I thought he was different, that he had honor. He has no honor." Ivan shook his head in sorrow. Guess his world had been blown apart same as mine.

I stared at him hard, looked into his soul and saw that he was telling the truth. I think I already knew deep down that he'd been on the level, but was looking for people to blame anywhere I could find them.

"Okay," I said, deflated, letting the magic recede, much to Wand's annoyance.

"I was gonna blast him good," said Wand, disappointed.

"Don't worry, there'll be plenty of bad guys to incinerate."

"Cool."

I put Wand away while I got funny looks from the others. Vicky and George understood, but Ivan stared at me like I'd lost my few remaining marbles.

"No, I wasn't talking to myself. It's a long story. Right, so what do we do now?" I asked Ivan.

"Now we sit down and have dinner with the girls, then later we talk."

I nodded, finally got around to saying hello to everyone properly, then the girls came rushing in and there was no chance to talk about much of anything as there were more important things to discuss. Like what so-and-so had said at school, and how it was like, really, really unfair that some girls had red hair like George, and I even had to show them the wand I'd finished, keeping quiet about it being sentient.

Belatedly, I got a chance to ask about George's day, and her face lit up. She showed us all the details for several properties, and I was impressed. I kept quiet, but one stood out for me from the rest, but we looked at everything and then I asked the girls what they preferred, which one they'd like to come and visit the most. They picked the same one as me. Yes. Then I asked George, and she said she agreed.

"Then it's settled. Let's buy it."

"Dad, you haven't even seen it yet."

"But you have, right? You went and had a snoop around?"

"Of course. And it was amazing. Ten acres, nearly all of it flat, and there's already stables for the horses. I'd just have to get fencing done and a place for training, but it's pretty nice."

"And the house, is it big, Aunty George?"

"Huge. And, and this is the best bit, it's got a massive barn attached to it that Dad can turn into his perfect kitchen."

"Really?" I asked, feeling the first bit of joy all day. I grabbed the details and looked through them properly. It was perfect. We could get the builders in, open up from the house into the barn, and have a kitchen the size of most regular houses. Awesome.

"It's ten minutes to the coast, only about fifteen from the, er, the 'gate,' so it'll hardly be like moving at all.

"But it's so far to travel," whined a sprog. "That's why we never came to visit you before. Can't you live close to us?"

"Don't you worry about that," I said in a whisper. "I know a magic way to get to Cornwall that will take no time at all."

"Arthur, you can't show them the... you-know-what, you can't."

"But they know I'm a wizard, know about George." I said nothing about their mum being a werewolf, their uncle being a vampire werewolf, but there was no way these kids wouldn't find out more about what we all got up to whether we wanted them to or not. They were smart and had already discovered more than we'd assumed. It was just a matter of time.

"Tell us, Uncle Arthur, tell us please?"

I looked to Vicky and she nodded with a sigh.

"I have a magic portal. It will take you from my house in the city to a barn in the country, then it's just a short drive to our new house. Actually, you've already been there. Remember last year when you came to stay?"

"But we fell asleep and you drove us there," said a fidgety bag of energy.

"Aha, or did you go through a magic portal?"

"Wow."

"That's so cool."

"I know, right?"

"So, we're going to buy it?" asked George.

"We sure are. Tomorrow. We'll buy it tomorrow. Make them a great offer, get it rushed through. I know a guy, he'll have us in within the week. Joint names on the property, yours and mine. Equal shares," I said to George.

"Except I don't have to put down half the money," she said morosely. "Because I can't."

I leaned over and whispered to Vicky. She nodded, eyes tearing up. She grabbed her laptop from the island and tapped away in her usual insane way, like she was trying to pound it into submission, then came back and sat down, grinning.

George's phone beeped and she checked it, even though there was a rule about no technology at the table. Her eyes widened and she looked up at me. "You did this?"

"Sure. So, now you have the money, still wanna go equal shares?"

"You bet. Thanks, Dad. That's, um, I don't know what to say."

"Say you'll always put the tea towels in the right drawer and stop messing up my cutlery."

"Promise."

We chatted some more and soon enough the girls were tucked up in bed and it was just the grown-ups. That's how I saw George now, and she'd be even more grown up once she heard what had gone on and what I had planned.

I wasn't sure whether to discuss it with Ivan, but he was part of this, and I had to trust him or I'd end up not even trusting my own family.

So, knowing it would hurt George, feeling like an awful man and worse father, I told them all what happened with Candy.

Ivan wasn't surprised, obviously, Vicky was aghast, and George, my darling daughter, she came and gave me a hug.

I love that girl more every day.

Schemes

"So that's how Mikalus knew exactly when to hit Cerberus? He was listening in on us, knew when we were doing our thing?" asked Vicky.

"Yeah," I said, feeling all kinds of depressed again. "And then I guess they tipped off Cerberus so they'd clear out the warehouse. Ugh, I hate all this sneaky shit, makes my head hurt."

"Dad, are you okay?" asked George, knowing how I'd felt about Candy, about how important it was I didn't involve her in my life with women, or usual lack of, unless I was sure of them. Shows how bad a judge of character I was.

"Honestly? No. I feel like the worst for what I did to Candy. I feel like a fool for trusting her, like an amateur for being bugged, and angry as hell for being played by Mikalus. Mostly I am so sad I want to curl up and cry." I could have done it too, could have found a dark room, huddled under the blankets, and stayed there for a lifetime. I wanted to hide and never see another living soul again.

"You've got us," said Vicky kindly. "Did he tell you what he did for me earlier?"

George nodded. Ivan raised an eyebrow.

"Dad's the best."

"You saved my sister, it's why I'm here. Plus I was betrayed the same as you."

"So what are we going to do about it?" I asked. I had a tentative plan but it wasn't exactly mind-blowing, and I could do with all the help I could get.

"We're going to destroy them. All of them," said Ivan, resolute.

"What do you mean all of them?" I knew he couldn't mean destroy Cerberus and the vampires, that wasn't possible, and he was a vampire.

"I mean exactly what I said. We'll ensure nothing like this ever happens again. All this scheming and backstabbing, it isn't how it's meant to be, how it should work. There will always be different sides, but this, it's not how you play the game." Ivan leaned back in his chair and laced his fingers behind his head. He was determined, he'd already made his mind up.

"So you're not going to suck it up, do what Mikalus tells you?"

"He made a fool out of me. I understand his reasons, that if I'd known I would have told you, and that's the point. He treated me like a kid, made me act against my will, and I will not stand for it. I spent a lifetime doing what I was told, acting in ways I found despicable, all because there was the promise of my sister being returned held over me. It was all a lie, a sham, and I can never get those years back. I will not be a puppet for someone who thinks they have the right to own me ever again. This stops now."

"That's what I wanted to hear."

"We are men of honor," said Ivan, looking about as scary as I'd ever seen him look.

"Honor," I agreed.

We talked late into the night, as a family, and finally, exhausted, we all went to bed in a smart guest bedroom, of which there were way too many.

Maybe in the morning the world would seem like a brighter place. I knew it wouldn't, but what is there without hope?

Normal? What's Normal

Ivan left early, not long after I finally crawled out of bed, fed up with lying there cursing life, mine in particular. He said that for now he'd act normal, go along with things and not kick up a fuss. It was what we'd agreed on and he was an infinitely patient man. There is nothing as deadly as an enemy who can bide their time. He wouldn't have long to wait though, neither would I.

Vicky and the girls bustled about, doing the usual manic morning routine involving cereal, arguments over the TV, bickering over whose socks were whose, and then they were out the door, leaving George and I in peace.

I'd forgotten what it was like having children around; it was exhausting. How any parent coped was a mystery. Now that was a real job. No wonder Vicky was always tired.

We spoke for a while about the mess we were currently in, and George asked if there was anything she could do. I told her no, that I didn't want her involved in this as it went beyond serious and was pretty much off the charts. She argued, said she was powerful in her own right now, could open Paths and do all kinds of awesome stuff, but I'd hear none of it. She was still learning, and there was a long way to go. The only thing I wanted her doing was sorting out the house.

It was an excuse, a way to keep her occupied. The further away from this she was the better. She said she'd go down to Cornwall again, make the offer, and get in touch with my guy who would speed the whole process through. With a few bribes in the right places, any property could be bought within a week, or less. She'd stay at a friend's in Mousehole, and I was so relieved I almost burst into tears.

We sorted through the clothes she'd bought for us the day before and, as expected, she'd done an incredible job. More of the same for me, as she knew what I liked and that I was averse to change, and then showed off some of her new things. She looked stunning and I told her so. Her neck flushed but she smiled happily and took the compliment as intended. Such an amazing woman. I didn't deserve her.

"I can't believe you're taking this so well," I said. "All your things are gone, our house. Everything. Aren't you sad?"

"Not really. You always told me, it's just stuff. There were a few items I would have liked to hold on to, but there's no point thinking about that now. It's all gone." And then she cried. And so I cried because she was sad, and because it was all my fault, and that no matter how much I blamed power-mad zealots or monomaniacal vampires, I'd still brought it all down on myself by getting involved with any of them in the first place.

"Don't blame yourself," she said, reading my mind. "They know the rules, we all do, and they broke them. Now it's our turn." She grinned, looking sinister as hell. I wouldn't want to mess with her.

"I'm glad you're my daughter."

"Me too."

George left soon after and I was alone for about the time it took to clean Vicky's kitchen so I didn't lose the plot, then Vicky returned.

She came into the kitchen, pulled the tea towel out of my hands without saying a word, and took my hand gently.

"What are you doing?" I asked as she dragged me through the kitchen and out into the hall.

Vicky put a finger to her lips and then pulled me up the stairs. What was this about? As we got closer to her bedroom, my stomach churned and I pulled back on her hand.

"No, Vicky, we can't."

"Just shut up." She tugged me into the bedroom, and I could have stopped her, but I let her lead me. She closed the door behind us.

"You need this. I need this. Let's do it."

And with that, Vicky took off her mom sweater, removed her jeans, peeled off socks bought from the kids' department, and stood there in lacy underwear, looking, well, she looked sexy.

I stripped, and before I knew it we were kissing. It was warm and wet and nice. Then we were naked, and on the bed, and then we did things I had never expected to do with Vicky.

Afterward, lying there on top of the covers, hot and sweaty, panting and avoiding looking at each other, the silence dragged on and on.

Finally, Vicky spoke. "Well, that was weird."

"Um, yeah, it was."

"Like, er, like sleeping with a friend. Almost like sleeping with a brother, but not in a gross incestuous way, just..."

"Just like it was friends sleeping together, but more. We're beyond that, we're family, even if not by blood."

Vicky propped herself up on one elbow and turned to me. "That's it! It was like we're family but not family. It was nice and all, but..."

"But we aren't suited that way. We have something else, something more important than sex."

"Family, and love."

"Family and love," I agreed.

And for a while, lying on oversized pillows in Vicky's ridiculous bedroom with way too many frills and too much pink, I think we both found something we'd been searching for our whole lives.

A moment of peace while all around was madness.

Things changed that day. Our relationship would never be the same. The weird thing is, it actually made it better. We'd never be a couple, never be lovers again, and we were closer because of it.

She'd always be annoying though. Some things were beyond even this mighty wizard to change. And part of me would never have it any other way.

Satan's Breath

Vicky and I stared at each other a little sheepishly for a while, and then we burst out laughing. We had to see the funny side of it, we really did. And I'm glad we did what we did. We'd got it out of the way, moved past it. I'm not even sure we fancied each other, just that we were so close, had gone through so much, lost so much, that we found solace in each other's arms, which was as it should have been.

Then we showered, got dressed, and went back downstairs.

"So, what's the plan?"

"The plan, my badly dressed diminutive devil, is to ensure that nobody screws with us again. Ivan will do whatever he does with Mikalus, and we'll get to Cerberus and make them wish they'd never heard of us."

"Yes!" Vicky did her embarrassing mom-jig as I rolled my eyes at her antics. I couldn't help but laugh. The absurdity of it all, what we'd done, her being annoying and over-excitable like a puppy after you've been out all day, me despairing.

Guess this was my future; maybe it wouldn't be so bad.

We finalized some details over coffee, going over what we'd agreed with Ivan the night before, talking about the plan we'd all formed late into the night, seeing if it held up to the saner daylight hours when your reasoning isn't as jaded and you can think more sharply.

It had plenty of holes in it, but it might just work.

Maybe.

What did we have to lose? We couldn't go on like this? Assassination attempts, bombs, it was ridiculous.

Then I left, content with the beefed-up security Ivan had arranged. There were more men than bloody flowers in the garden; Vicky would be fine.

I drove to the city, feeling out of place and time, head swimming with plans and indecision, concern and worry about the whole sorry enterprise, but knowing I'd been pushed to the limits and this had to be resolved.

I let it all fall aside as I pulled up outside a familiar building sat incongruously amid the wasteland of a once thriving area of commerce. Most properties were cracked and crumbling, slowly decaying.

But Satan's Breath endured, proud and indomitable, the boxy exterior giving no hint as to what awaited inside.

I pushed through the doors, held back as the Turk had a conversation with an old wizard every member recognized and dreaded encountering in the locker room. The ball-sack dryer extraordinaire. This had been going on for years now, the Turk finally having got around to having a word with him last year, but the complaints continued and the old guy seemed unable to understand why other wizards didn't want to share the same space as him while he stood naked with his leg up on a sink and blow-dried his hairy, wrinkled, way too old to ever be exposed, nether regions under a force-nine gale as he heated his nuts until close to roasting.

"But I have to get it all dry down there," the wizened old man whined.

"Use a towel, it's what they're for. I don't even charge," said the Turk, pointing to the collection behind him, all neatly rolled up, some even still looking white.

"They're all rough on my bits. I like the hairdryer. It does a better job and keeps me sprightly." The old-timer did a little jig then jumped and clicked his heels together.

"I don't care," said the Turk, wiping sweat off his brow with his stained white vest, exposing a very large and hairy belly. "I've been getting complaints, again, and people are refusing to come if they know you're here. Either you stop it or you're banned." The Turk folded his meaty forearms across his barrel chest and stared down at the old guy.

"Fine, but it's your fault if I get a nasty infection or disease and they fall off."

"I'll take full responsibility if it all suddenly detaches due to lack of exposure to warm g-forces."

"Can I go in now?"

"Hand it over first." The Turk held out a hand and the grumbling wizard reluctantly fished about in his bag then pulled out a hairdryer that looked older than him. He passed it over like he was giving away his last coin, and his shoulders sagged.

"Spoilsport."

"Here's a towel, you fruitcake." The Turk handed over a towel and the wizard wandered off, muttering to himself.

I stepped up to the small counter and grinned at the owner of the finest sauna in the country, mainly because it was wizards only, no women or citizens allowed. And very, very hot. "About time," I said, as the Turk wrote my name in his book.

"It's weird," he said, scratching his mustache, thicker than a broom and twice as tough.

"Sure is." I took my towel, nodded, then went into the locker room.

The place was quiet at this time of day, but would get busier later when the wizards emerged from their festering pits. It was just me and the old guy, who changed quickly then shuffled off into the pool area.

I checked the wards on my locker, more out of habit than anything else. They were as secure as ever. With tingly fingers, I dropped the wards, put up a veil just to ensure nobody could see what was inside if they were snooping, then opened the metal locker. All of us had a similar setup. Satan's Breath was more secure than a bank vault so most had goodies stashed, and privacy was never a problem as we respected each other but it always paid to be careful.

The door opened and magical emanations hit, but I ignored them, dismissed the pleadings of dangerous books and the mutterings of statuettes, and just smiled at the last remaining items I owned in the whole world. These were the ones that mattered, that I would be sorry to see go. One in particular was very important at the moment, would allow me to do what I intended, follow this path until its end, no matter what.

"You sure this is a good idea?" asked Wand, sounding slightly panicked.

"Absolutely. Not."

"Remember what I said about focusing. You can't screw this up. Nobody else even knows this is a possibility, so don't let me down."

"I'll try not to," I said, feeling slightly panicked.

I reached out and grabbed the Teleron.

Resolute

I focused like I'd never focused before, did as Wand had instructed, following his guidelines to the letter, and pictured my destination with a clarity that became almost frightening, building up the image until it felt real enough to touch.

Nerves tried to surface but I shoved them down, refused to let emotion play a part in this. I had one chance, and one chance only, to get this right. If I screwed up I was done for, and Death would be waiting. I could picture him sitting at his desk, rubbing his hands together as he got ready to put a line through my name, maybe for the last time.

A black rectangle popped into existence in the narrow space between the rows of lockers. Infinite, dark, and deadly.

"Game on, bitches."

I stepped through.

War

Pain engulfed me as it always did, but it was so brief it vanished almost as soon as it registered. As I stepped through, I pulled Wand from my pocket and asked, "You ready for this?"

"I was born ready."

"So was I." I decided conclusively that I liked him. He was my kinda sentient stick.

My will was streaming down my arm and powering up Wand even as the portal closed behind me. Carmichael and three huge Hounds, men with thick beards and chiseled cheekbones like they'd stepped right out of Greek history, turned at the sound of the magic fizzing as the sigils activated and Wand leaked.

"Hey, don't go off prematurely," I whispered.

"Sorry, it's exciting, and I'm new to this. I'll be able to last longer once I get in more practice."

I sighed. Last thing I needed was a premature magical ejaculation, but I sensed his power, the throbbing in my hand, and felt a little icky because of it.

Anyway, no time to worry about that now. As shock registered on the faces of the Hounds, I let rip. Or Wand and I did. I wasn't sure who was doing the work as my hand lifted and waved as if of its own volition, slicing Wand through the air, thrusting forward to point at each man in turn. The Hounds were hit within less than a second.

They kind of exploded. Okay, they did explode.

"You were supposed to frazzle them, not burst them," I complained.

"What's the difference?" asked Wand, giving off a deep sense of satisfaction as the sigils dulled and his thoughts, words, unspoken telepathic conversation, whatever it was, receded along with the ebbing magic.

"A big one," I muttered, then focused my attention on the one man remaining upright in front of me. Carmichael was covered head to toe in gore. He was drenched in blood, had gobbets of flesh stuck to his tweed jacket, and for some reason didn't seem pleased to see me. He stared at me hard, not so much surprised as resigned, and then he did the strangest thing.

Without breaking eye contact, he smoothed a slender hand across his face, smearing the blood, then licked his finger.

"Fuck, I forgot."

And I had, sort of. I mean, I knew he was a vampire, but he was so unlike a vampire that it hadn't sunk in, not like it had with Ivan and Mikalus. He was a posh twat in tweed with a perfect haircut, full of presence, unlike every other vampire I'd met. Had rigid military bearing and a smug self-awareness, and I couldn't reconcile this man with being a bloodsucker.

But he was, and the facade was down. Carmichael's teeth snicked down in the most worrying of ways, and he licked his finger again, tongue running around lips now engorged with blood. He sighed as his eyes clouded over then became bloodshot. The pupils dilated and he grinned at me, not in a nice way.

"Hey, Carmichael, so not nice to see you again."

"You're a hard man to kill," he said, rolling his head until his neck clicked.

"No, you did a fine job. Actually, you killed me twice, but you know how it goes."

"Not really, but no matter, you're here now. I believe you have something that belongs to me." Carmichael nodded at the Teleron held tight in my hand.

"Why don't you come get it?" I asked.

"Maybe I will." Carmichael turned to the boffins in the room, an operations center by the seems of it. They were all still in their chairs, looking freaked. Some were crying. Men and women stared aghast at the lumps of meat on the floor, then glanced back at their screens where they seemed to be viewing places from a great height. "You can all leave."

They moved to stand but I growled, "Wait," and they stayed put. "Drone operatives?" I asked Carmichael.

"Amongst other things. Surveillance, data harvesting, things of that nature."

"The modern age, eh?"

"Yes, it's quite something, isn't it?"

"Yeah. And do they know what they are involved in?"

"They know."

Before he'd even finished speaking, Wand spat volatile fire gathered from the very air itself, sucking oxygen into a vortex around the workers, making the tiniest of sparks within the electrical currents cause an inferno. They were blasted into atoms immediately, and the room turned blinding white as banks of monitors, the cages full of servers, workstations, and who knew what else, was consumed by fire.

Apart from me, because I knew what I was doing and wasn't in the mood to play nice. I was wrapped up safe and sound in a cocoon of protection, leaving me standing unharmed as the world disintegrated around me. I was surprised by my own power, as by rights I should have been running on empty by now. The only thing I could assume was that Wand was drawing on power I myself didn't possess, which was kinda neat.

When the fire died as quickly as it had started, chunks of metal, brick, concrete, and bodies littered the room, or what was left of it. The destruction was complete, only stopping three feet away, piled high like a wall of flesh and steel. The walls were mostly blown out, revealing a corridor on one side and lo and behold, a new warehouse on the other.

"Nice," I said, turning to Carmichael. "Wasn't expecting it to be this easy."

He was naked, burned black, skin already blistering, peeling away to reveal fresh pink flesh beneath. His hair was gone, scalp like lava, but it was growing back and he was still standing.

Things got ugly after that.

The Lion's Den

"It's not possible," growled Carmichael through the blackened hole that was his mouth. His lips were gone, just large blisters that oozed as he spoke, but they were growing back fast. Trust me, it was gross. Like a puckered anus talking, which is utterly disconcerting.

"Surprise," I said, grinning.

Sirens wailed, lights flashed red in the corridor, people rushed past, and Hounds amassed. The massive storage room, the new warehouse, was lit up like they'd never heard of energy-saving bulbs.

"How did you get here?" he asked, voice raw even though most of him had recovered by now.

"You know how. Used your Teleron." I bet he hated that. It was his, and now it would be his downfall. Although, I was surprised it had worked. All credit to Wand. I never would have thought of it myself, or risked it. But Wand was right, and about the scrubbers too. There weren't any. Backup locations are never as secure, but it was still a major risk.

"But... but you've never been here," he wailed.

"Careful, Carmichael, you're losing your twat-like calm, getting all stressy. It's bad for your blood pressure, you know?"

Carmichael glared at me, not looking smarmy and dapper any longer, instead looking deranged and dangerous. He was annoyed as hell, and couldn't figure it out, so maybe I'd share, just to piss him off.

"I've got you in my sights, buddy. I can jump to anywhere you are. I got it figured out. I don't have to picture a place to get it to work, I can picture you instead."

"Liar! That's not how it works." And with that he sprinted for me. His flesh split at the knees and elbows, the new skin so tight it wasn't prepared for such exertions. He screamed in agony as his body was torn apart once more.

Wand moved without me even having to think, and the room exploded with white light once more, throwing Carmichael back and away, a true Second but I was beating him down. Goes to show how important the element of surprise is. But he was vampire and I'd never fought one as powerful as this, so didn't know what to expect.

I didn't have to wait long.

He slammed into what remained of the wall leading to the warehouse. Brick and concrete rained down, denting flesh and cutting him to shreds, but he was up in an instant, his mangled body recovering before my eyes, and then he was coming for me again. Wand blasted, but Carmichael raised a hand and the magic spread and bounced off, a shield protecting him.

He careened into me and I went down, but I already had a protective bubble of my own wrapped tight to my skin so no damage done.

Hounds were everywhere now, cramming into the room, unable to do anything because Carmichael and I were tangled tight. The sirens grew louder, the lights brighter, flashing incessantly as Carmichael tried to strangle me. I felt nothing even though he was shaking my head like a rag doll's.

So I kicked him in the nuts. Works every time.

Carmichael's grip loosened and this ancient vampire gasped as I shucked him off easily, using the precious second I had before Hounds got their act together to run to the trashed wall and clamber through. I took in the sight of the warehouse, focused like I'd never focused before, and tried to imprint an image of it in my mind.

"Remember," I said, turning as Carmichael got to his feet and the Hounds crowded around. "Anywhere, any time, I can come get you. Watch your back, dickhead." And with that I twisted the Teleron and stepped back through the portal I knew was behind me but not even checking, wanting to make a cool exit and all.

Back in Satan's Breath I brushed at my dusty clothes, took Grace off and cleaned her up, and although I knew I'd regret it, I peeked around the edge of the lockers because I heard a familiar humming sound.

"What the fuck is wrong with you?" I asked the old dude standing naked with his leg up on the row of sinks, hairdryer blowing at his balls like two battered walnuts in an old pair of tights.

He grinned at me and carried on his despicable act.

I shook my head and returned to my locker, carried on counting in my head.

I hurriedly grabbed a few artifacts from my locker and finished the countdown. "Nine, ten," I said out loud, then twisted the Teleron once again and walked through the portal.

Guess Who's Back?

Infinite bags are extremely useful, especially when you go on holiday. They're also cool for going to the supermarket, as you don't get caught short and have to pay for a plastic one—curse my impulsive shopping habits. They're also a right royal pain in the ass as you can imagine how long it takes to find anything.

Nevertheless, the moment I stepped through the portal into the far reaches of this new warehouse, I opened the fastener of the bag that looked like something Mary Poppins would love for Christmas, an old-fashioned thing made of thick wool, like a knitting bag with robust leather handles.

Things made weird noises in the crates I was surrounded by, but rather than dwell on them too much, or consider how wise a course of action this was, I pulled out Wand and asked, "You ready for this?"

The bag growled.

"Damn, forgot that was in there. Oh well. And I was talking to Wand. Wand, you ready?"

"Sure am," he said, sounding way too excited. Guess it was all new to him and he was eager for the experience. Magic was brimming with such potency I felt like he could go off at any moment, so it was now or never.

"Give it all you've got," I whispered, crouching low so nobody at the other end of the warehouse, where there was still one hell of a commotion, would see. I could already hear jackboots marching though the warehouse, Carmichael obviously having had the presence of mind to get the place secured as fast as possible.

But not fast enough.

I tapped Wand on the open lip of the bag and the air shimmered above it. Then I turned to the closest rack, held Wand loosely, and said, "Get 'em in quick."

Energy surged and Wand went to work.

Crates small and large flew through the air, aiming right at the bag. Just before they reached it they wobbled as though in a mirage and shrank so they'd fit through the mouth. In they went, one after the other, faster and faster as Wand got into his stride, using the most efficient route possible to get the artifacts stashed.

I began to sweat as the magic drained out of me, until my whole body was shaking and my teeth chattered. This was a massive outpouring of energy and magic always has to come from somewhere. Wand was using amplified air currents and any residual energy he could draw on to power his work, and although lights were dimming and the room hummed with the thievery of energy, I was also using a lot of my own.

Things worsened rapidly and I had to sit down, letting Wand take over, move my hand to point at a crate and drag it through the vibrating air then release it above the bag. But the work continued unabated, so fast everything was a blur.

There were shouts and loud footsteps; time was almost up. Wand went into overdrive, emptying racks in seconds, and with a final surge of magic I pushed out the bubble of protection until it took in maybe a third of the warehouse itself, right up to the fast-approaching Hounds.

I grimaced, but waved at the men as they came up hard against the barrier. Then I spied Carmichael pushing through the Hounds, looking severely pissed off.

"I told you not to fuck with me. You broke the Code," I shouted, but I don't know if he heard me or not. He shouted at his men as crates flew overhead then disappeared into the bag. But Wand was slowing, I was close to unconscious, and my arm began to drop.

"That's enough, time to go," I whispered.

"We got 'em, we got 'em good."

"Sure did."

I twisted the Teleron and a portal appeared in front of us. Carefully, I got to my feet, lowered the protective barrier, and as Hounds rushed forward I locked eyes with Carmichael and said, "You really screwed up. Nobody fucks with The Hat."

I picked up the infinite bag and stepped through the portal.

One More Go

I was pushing my luck, and to be honest was amazed I'd managed to jump to Carmichael, let alone managed another to the warehouse, but I was in the zone and so determined, so focused, that I got the feeling I could have gone to the moon if I'd wanted. I probably would have tried it too, but my spacesuit was at the dry cleaners.

Weak of knee, yet strong of heart, I shoved the infinite bag into my locker, checked I had the other item I had yet to use, slammed the door shut, put up my wards as this was too precious a haul to trust my fellow wizards with, and activated the Teleron once again.

I stepped through and grabbed Carmichael around the neck, inches away from an alarming number of Hounds. What worried me most was that Wand was in my pocket and out of reach as I held the Teleron in my left hand and had Carmichael head-locked in my right with a knife at his throat. If this went wrong I was screwed, but I had a bargaining chip now, or a third of a warehouse full of bargaining chips.

"Tell them to back off," I whispered intimately into Carmichael's ear. "I won't count to five. You've got one second." I wasn't joking, I would have slit his throat so deep his head would fall off in a heartbeat, and I'd like to see him come back from that, vampire or not.

"Move away," ordered Carmichael, the words coming out raspy as his body recovered from the fire damage.

The Hounds obeyed instantly, fanning out and forming a circle around us a few steps distant.

"Tell them to move away from the wall," I ordered.

"Move away from the wall," said Carmichael.

After the Hounds had moved, I walked forward with Carmichael still held fast. Close to the wall, I turned to face into the room and backed up until I felt brick against my heels.

"Now, everyone take five steps away. We wouldn't want any accidents, now would we? Oh, and as a friendly reminder, if anyone tries anything, I'll kill Carmichael immediately. And if you kill me, you'll never get the artifacts back. Understand?" They glared at me. "Understand?" I shouted.

There were nods and grunts. If looks could kill, I'd have definitely used up my remaining lives, however many there were.

"What do you want?" croaked Carmichael, who was being sensible and moving as little as possible.

"What I want is to set the record straight. You willing to do that, give me a minute of your time?"

"Do I have a choice?"

"Sure you do," I said without malice. "You can agree, or we can carry on like this for a while. I can come back any time I want and you'll never see me coming. You want to play dirty then so be it. This is playing dirty. You overstepped the line, now I want this finished."

"You tricked us, you had it coming."

"I was going to steal some books, Mikalus' books, and sure, I knew that would piss you off. But I got played. Mikalus used me as a decoy. He betrayed me, betrayed Ivan, and my guess is he took a lot more than just a few books?"

Carmichael nodded.

"Right, so he beat us both, got you to move the warehouse so he could grab what he wanted. Leaving me to get slaughtered. But guess what? I'm still alive, even after you dropped a fucking bomb on my daughter. And then you tried to assassinate Vicky. Have you no shame?"

Carmichael tried to turn but I increased the pressure on the knife. He groaned but stopped moving. "Vicky? I had nothing to do with that. She's got young children, and much as I'd like her out of the picture I swear I ordered no such thing. Unless my boss did, then it wasn't us. We aren't monsters."

I believed him. What would be the point in lying about it?

"Do not move," I ordered. Carefully, I pocketed the Teleron and pulled my phone out of my pocket. I called Vicky and she answered. "Hello?"

"Have you got it?" I asked.

"Easy peasy. I've got your exact location. You're a few hours away, but I know exactly where you are."

"Good. Call Ivan, tell him I'm on my way." I hung up.

"So you know where you are, so what?"

"So it means that if you try to move the rest of the warehouse, I'll know, and I'll tell every fucking wizard in the country that you're on the move with trucks full of magical artifacts. How d'you think that will go down? This may have all gone to shit, but I can come here any time now, and if you move it then you're gonna lose what little you have left. You were safe in the city, we couldn't get in easily, could never get away with so much, plus I didn't want to, knew it would cause too much trouble, but now..."

"Now what?"

"Now I'm pissed off. Now we can keep an eye on you, and if you move the artifacts I swear you'll be finished. And if you come after me again, you'll never get back what I took. But mostly, I just want to know George and Vicky and her kids will be safe."

"We'll find what you took, you know we will."

"Maybe, but it won't be easy. Vicky's already set things up so if anything happens to me this location gets sent to every magic user in the country. Nobody believed you lot would be stupid enough to keep everything in one place like you do, but once they know they'll be all over you. You had to push too far, didn't you?"

"We thought you'd tricked us. We don't like being tricked. We lost a lot."

"Not my problem. Now, say goodbye."

I felt Carmichael stiffen, ready himself for death, but he didn't know the half of it. I twisted the Teleron, felt the energy change as a portal opened behind us, and stepped back not against the wall, but through space-time itself.

This was getting tiring, but I couldn't stop, not now.

Bit Spooky

We fell back through the portal and I watched, squinting in the weak light as it contracted to a single point of emptiness then popped out of existence. Although I was falling, and my instinct was to reach behind to cushion the blow, I didn't. I kept a firm hand on the Teleron, knowing it would be very bad to lose it, and with the other I maintained my tight grip on Carmichael, the knife dangerously close to his throat as we toppled. He'd just have to deal with a slight nick if it came to that.

I hit with a thud, and it hurt like hell, but Carmichael was wriggling a little so he wasn't dead. I was a little disappointed but knew I had to stick to the plan, not succumb to my darker side. If Carmichael croaked it, he'd only be replaced, and I'd be right back at square one. Much as it went against my few principles and better judgment, as revenge is sweet, I knew I had to forge a relationship with this man, get order to my life, and Cerberus constantly at my back wasn't going to let that happen.

Plus, and I smiled in the half-light at the thought, I had a very special meeting arranged for my vampire friend here.

Speaking of which.

The lights flicked on and standing over us, naked, and looking all kinds of awesome, was Mikalus.

"Guess it worked then," I said, groaning as my knees grated while I got awkwardly to my feet, still holding on to Carmichael. His neck was bloodied, and he had a few gashes from the knife, but nothing too deep. The wounds were already healing.

"You are intruding," said Mikalus, looking weak and sleepy, hair tousled but still shining and salon fresh. He visibly powered-up as he came around from the sleep he'd obviously been deeply in. His muscles filled out, he seemed to grow leaner and more defined, and took on a vitality that was a little unnerving.

Plus he was naked, and two naked men in a room, plus me, made me feel uncomfortable. Especially when they both wanted me dead and were vampires.

Funny what can stress a guy out.

"And you're going to go get some clothes on. You too," I said, pushing Carmichael away from me, keeping a firm grip on the Teleron. I thought better of it, so swapped it to my left, pocketed the knife, and grabbed Wand.

He gave a cheery, "This is exciting," as I pulled him out. I got the weirdest sensation, like he was taking a look around the room, but surely he could see wherever he was, if he could see at all? I'd have to ask. Another time, maybe?

Mikalus was cool and relaxed, did nothing but raise an eyebrow at the state of Carmichael, then wandered off and returned a moment later with two silk dressing gowns. Black, obviously. I couldn't imagine them wearing white fluffy numbers with matching slippers.

Carmichael took the dressing gown and both men covered themselves up. Then we did a bit of staring at each other, waiting for the other to say something first. I took the opportunity to check out the penthouse suite at vampire headquarters, and to say it was odd is an understatement. The room was almost empty.

There was an antique table with heavy wooden chairs, and a large TV on the wall. The only other feature was a series of dark oak bookcases along the opposite wall, easily fifty feet in length, crammed with books. More were piled up on the floor. Several crates from the warehouse were stacked on top of each other, presumably housing the rest, or maybe other items taken from Cerberus.

Finally, I turned back to the vampires, each at opposite poles of the magical community, and I said, "Here's how this is going to work."

"You don't give me orders," said Carmichael, looking almost, but not quite, taken aback.

"Or me."

"Today I do. Today I make the rules, and if either of you don't like them then you can pay the consequences."

"And what would they be?" asked Mikalus, amused.

Carmichael already knew, and I was pretty sure he'd leave me alone for a while, but he'd be after me eventually, same as always, so this had to work. Mikalus had no reason not to just kill me now, so I'd better give him one, and fast.

This was where the plan let me down. I was surprised I'd got this far, and had decided to wing it from here on.

Sometimes I curse my impulsive nature.

Laying Down the Law

"I want what you took from Cerberus." I stared hard at Mikalus, showing him my resolve, that I wasn't kidding. In fact, I didn't merely stare hard, I glared—super intimidating. He was quaking on the spot. I wasn't scared of him, not at this moment. I was all out of options, all out of energy. All I had left was hope and the need for this to be over.

"Haha, Arthur, you are a determined young man, but I don't answer to you, or him." Mikalus scowled at Carmichael who was looking at a bit of a loss in the middle of the room, clearly thinking what to do.

"Here's what will happen. I already have plenty of artifacts from the warehouse. Carmichael," I turned to him as I spoke his name, "you get them back eventually, a few here and there. That way you will keep out of my business and leave me and mine alone. A truce. No more interfering in each other's affairs. Agreed?"

Carmichael took a moment to mull it over, but he knew I had him beat, knew I was serious. Was killing me worth the risk? He'd had his revenge, or as close to it as he was going to get. It was time to draw a line under all of this.

"Well? I don't have all day."

"Agreed. If you give us the artifacts back at an arranged time each month, then we have a truce. I won't interfere in your business if you don't interfere in ours."

"It's a deal. And Mikalus, you have a lot to answer for. They almost killed my daughter. They shot Vicky! They dropped a bomb on my fucking house!" My anger was returning, rising like a dark tide, and Wand crackled with menace as magic readied to blast the hell out of this traitor.

"It was business," said Mikalus, showing just how cold a creature he was. Had he always been like this? Or was it the vampire nature that had made him become such an abomination?

"Business!? You cheated me, broke the Code."

"You refused to work for me any longer. This was my way of getting more use out of you. I knew the debt you owed Ivan, but I also knew you wouldn't be able to resist such a job. Your own greed got you involved in this. You could have said no."

"You're wrong. Unlike you, I'm a man of honor. I owed Ivan a debt and repaid it. You took advantage. You cheated me and you betrayed Ivan. You dishonored him."

There was a peculiar, extended knock at the door, a special combination prearranged. Without asking permission, I wandered over, acting casual even as my heart beat fast, and unlocked the door. Ivan nodded grimly at me and I glanced left then right in the hall, saw the dead goons, and raised an eyebrow.

"I dealt with most of the ones I could find in the building that were awake," whispered Ivan, then he strode past me.

This wasn't part of the plan, although we didn't have much of one to begin with. He was supposed to come, but not kill a load of Mikalus' goons. With a sigh, I closed the door behind us.

"What's the meaning of this?" asked Mikalus, indignant at the intrusion.

"This is me helping a friend who you betrayed. You have shamed me, I am no longer beholden to you."

"I am your maker. You belong to me."

"I belong to nobody. I did once, but never again. I loved you, you were my family. You used me to get what you wanted and didn't care about the consequences. You made me break my word, my honor." Ivan turned away from Mikalus and faced Carmichael. "And you, you tried to kill my friends and family. I understand your reason, but Vicky? Why did you attack my sister?" Ivan practically bristled with uncaged menace as he stepped toward Carmichael.

"I already told Arthur, we had nothing to do with Vicky. Not as far as I know, anyway. We attacked Arthur, he had it coming, regardless of if he'd been cheated or not, but Vicky? No."

Ivan paused, stared at Carmichael for the longest time, then whirled on Mikalus, enraged.

This wouldn't be pretty. Ivan was strong, but this was the original vampire. We had to follow what we'd discussed, which was to somehow take Mikalus' books and artifacts and make him behave, leave us alone. But Ivan wasn't in the mood for me to remind him about that.

And besides, it was his sister, and Mikalus had it coming.

Ivan stormed over and asked, "You? You had my sister targeted? Why?"

"Because she works for Arthur. We have to eliminate her, she is too capable. Her skills put us at risk. I knew she'd find a way to do us harm. This digital age is an annoyance." Mikalus scratched at his stubble like this was merely a slight interruption to his sleep. It drove Ivan wild.

He reached out and grabbed for Mikalus but Mikalus swatted him away like a fly. Backhanded him, sending Ivan flying across the room and smashing into the wall.

"Goddammit, I had a plan." I shouted as Wand spasmed and my arm lifted.

Sometimes I even lie to myself.

Vampire Melee

"No," I ordered Wand when sigils flared and my arm vibrated as magic surged even though I hadn't willed it.

"Why not? He just whacked your buddy."

"Because if I, or you, do anything too stupid, we'll never have peace."

I felt rather than heard Wand sigh with disappointment, but I knew I was right. That going after Mikalus physically wouldn't do me much good. Maybe I could beat him, maybe I couldn't, and that was the problem. I didn't know what he was capable of. Even if I destroyed him, I couldn't see it panning out well in the future. If I killed him then what? If I tried, and failed, then obviously I'd be in serious trouble as he didn't seem like the type of immortal vampire to take kindly to physical attacks.

No, better to just take what he'd stolen and make him promise to behave, leave me alone like Carmichael had vowed. I'd have his books, and would make a similar deal. He could have them back over time, if he kept his word.

Sure, there were more holes in this hasty plan than in a colander, but to be honest I was more concerned about Cerberus. Not that I didn't want to blast Mikalus to hell. I did. Basically, the whole thing was flakier than Vicky's pastry and a lot messier.

Ivan smashed into the floorboards with a force that would have broken any citizen's bones. Plaster and dust rained down on him as he lay in a heap, a huge dent in the wall. He leapt to his feet, face a mask of anger, the vampire fully in control. His eyes were dark, the pupils huge, the whites bloodshot. His usually thin lips were engorged with blood and his canines were long and deadly. He looked insane. Imagine coming across a feral man who'd lived in the woods his whole life and was caught in the act of tearing a rabbit to shreds with his teeth. And you stole it from him and began poking him with a sharp stick. He looked like that, but more annoyed and bewildered.

Mikalus stormed across the room, scowling, with similar vampiric attributes. You wouldn't want to get between these two, that was for sure.

So, with a sigh, I did exactly that.

I stepped forward just before Mikalus reached me, and put a hand out. "Let's not get carried away here. Mikalus, you deserve to be chopped up into tiny pieces and then hacked apart again as you regenerate for what you've done. It's one thing cheating me, making Ivan do it, but to go after the family of one of your own? That's stone-cold."

Mikalus glared at Ivan, ignoring me. "You dare lay a hand on me? Me, the First? Your master? You dare?" He spat his words, his teeth ripping his lips apart as he spoke. Blood sprayed onto the floor as he eyed Ivan with pure hatred.

"You deserve no respect," replied Ivan angrily. "You betrayed me. You used me and cast me aside even while you brought me closer. I thought you cared."

"Cared? Ha," laughed Mikalus. "You know nothing of caring. I have a world of my own kind to look after. My flock needs me. See how we have thrived since I returned? How they have new purpose and our presence has grown? You think you are important? You are not. Your friendship with this man," he pointed at me with a taloned finger that looked sharper than my blade, "is a disgrace. He is nothing but a wizard. A scruffy wizard."

"Charming," I said, grinning at Mikalus.

"See? A fool. And your sister, she will seek revenge. A distraction to your work, to our true purpose. She has to go. Maybe you shouldn't have shared such information, that she was your sister, with me."

"I told you because I trusted you, wanted her protected."

By now the two men were mere feet from each other, glaring and shaking. I was still between them, and I felt about as safe as a lobster wandering around the edge of the pool at Satan's Breath as a roomful of hungry wizards eyed it up.

I stepped aside, knowing I was probably making things worse. Plus not wanting to be eaten or anything.

"If I may?" interjected Carmichael. Everyone turned at the words; we'd all forgotten he was there.

"What?" snapped Ivan.

"Maybe we can all agree to let bygones be bygones? Put this behind us? We play our games, have been at war for so long, and where has it got us? We will never see things the same way, but maybe, just maybe, we can make an agreement that will give all sides peace. At least for the foreseeable future. How does that sound?"

Ivan paused to think, I could see the indecision on his face. He knew what he was getting into by confronting Mikalus like this, and the chances of him surviving were slim. Maybe he'd take the offer. He was wavering, and it sounded good to me. This kind of crap was why I didn't sleep well at night, and I'd had enough heartache.

My thoughts turned to Candy and her betrayal. I wanted to blame Mikalus for that, but knew I couldn't, not really. She'd made her choice same as we all make our own choices.

"No," said Mikalus. "You are as me, from a different time, Carmichael, and this new world does not have room for both of us. Eventually you will die, and I will be there to witness your downfall. I own this world, I will have it for me and mine. You should come to us, we may accept you. But if you remain with your Hounds then I have neither place, nor need, for you."

That sounded rather final, and I can't say I was shocked. Carmichael looked genuinely saddened, but he accepted the rebuff, smoothed his hair, stood tall and straight, and somehow even owned the fact he was in the middle of this madness wearing a borrowed dressing gown.

Mikalus was the same, proud and strong, able to ooze power and might whilst looking like he was about to go take a shower.

Ivan roared and charged Mikalus.

The dick.

It's Personal

Carmichael and I jumped aside as the two men went for each other. It was like they'd gone feral. I'd seen Ivan crackle and pop and turn into a bloody werewolf, but that was like a kid's bedtime story compared to this. I knew vampires could be wild; this was a whole other level.

As the blood flew and the injuries worsened, all I could do was stare in horror and astonishment at the damage the men inflicted on each other. Carmichael remained aloof, but his body was trembling and his eyes were dark. A single line of blood trickled from the corner of his mouth, and I caught a glint of white from his extended teeth even though he was trying to hide it. At that moment, I wondered how it was he managed to be out during daylight hours. That was something that would have saved Mikalus a lot of grief. Guess when you have access to untold artifacts there's bound to be one that could help, plus he knew a lot of magic.

Carmichael held his position though, and his cool. He was one hardcore dude, I'll give him that. There was no way I could intervene, they moved so fast and were so ferocious that I'd end up blasting Ivan. Plus, if I'm being truthful, I was worried I wouldn't finish Mikalus off and then I'd have his wrath descend. Ivan was being stupid, this wasn't the way things were meant to go, and he was risking everything. Even if Mikalus was killed, there'd be a hundred thousand vampires baying for his blood. It was a lose-lose situation.

But then the men broke. Mikalus was naked now, the dressing gown ripped off, and Ivan's clothes were in tatters. Both men looked like they'd been attacked by a pack of wild animals. Their faces were torn, huge welts where flesh was scratched or bitten away. Both were sticky with blood and Ivan had a huge tear in his chest, revealed where the shirt had been raked away.

Mikalus was faring just as poorly, if not worse. His muscular body was covered in sweat, and he'd lost most of a pectoral, the muscle ripped clean off. His left bicep was hanging, and his hands were bloodied. Flesh dropped from between his elongated fingernails.

I made a decision.

"I'll do it," I said to Ivan. And with that I raised Wand and against my better judgment I readied to do my best to defeat the original vampire.

"No," he gasped. "This is personal."

I nodded.

Sometimes a man has to stand up for what he feels is right, even if it means he'll die.

The men stared at each other for seconds that felt like minutes as their bodies repaired. Then they screamed and charged each other once again.

Feeling Left Out

"The outcome changes nothing," I shouted across the room to Carmichael who was eyeing the bookshelves greedily, obviously wondering how he could take everything and get out of here. I knew he wouldn't try to fight me, he wasn't that stupid. He was no Mikalus, didn't have his power. Maybe not being the true First meant he was more akin to a Second even though he'd been made in much the same way. But I saw it in his eyes, the hunger for the books, the decision not to fight me one-on-one.

"It will change everything," he shouted as Ivan and Mikalus tore each other apart. "If Ivan dies, you have one less ally. But our agreement stands, I made a promise."

"You good for your word, are you? I don't believe it." I jumped aside as the two men rolled right at my legs, gouging each other's eyes and generally having all the fun.

"I am a man of honor too, although you may not believe it. This is not how I like to do business, all this subterfuge. But so be it." He appeared appalled by the bloody scene before us and what had led to it.

Could he truly be a man of his word? I didn't care, I had his stuff. But I was growing increasingly sickened by the way my friend and my enemy were destroying each other. How could they endure so much?

As if reading my mind, both men broke apart and retreated to opposite ends of the room where they crouched and eyed each other warily. Both were utterly exhausted and their recovery took longer. It was minutes while their flesh healed and even then it was imperfectly. Ivan's torso was bare now, his shirt and jacket nothing but rags strewn around the room, stuck to the floor, walls, and ceiling by his own blood. His body was criss-crossed with scars new and old, as if his past had come back to haunt him in his weakened state and the flesh had memory of all he'd endured over his sorrow-filled existence.

Mikalus was just as ruined. His body was covered in bruises, purple and dark blotches against his pale skin. Skin that had never seen the light of day, had never felt the joy of the sun on his body.

Then I had an idea. And it wasn't a good one, it wasn't a sensible one, but I was all out of options. Ivan was going to get himself killed, that was obvious. Then what? I could leave, I had the Teleron, but after? Would Mikalus let this lie? Even if I took his books? No, this had gone too far now, he'd do all he could to wipe me out, and everyone I loved.

Wand tingled in my hand where I'd been holding him the entire time, and we made a silent pact to do this thing. My arm rose and I watched as time slowed and my mind processed information at a faster rate. I caught the expression on Carmichael's face and he smiled, knowing what I was about to do.

Then Mikalus glanced up, saw my arm arc, and where I was pointed, and uncertainty crossed his face. Ivan noticed the change in atmosphere and whispered, "Do it."

I nodded at him, said "Goodbye, motherfucker," to Mikalus, and Wand burst free with stored magical energy. A deadly jet of destruction aimed at the outer wall, a wall that was the only thing stopping the daylight shining into this room.

Ancient vampires don't like the sun, it makes them ashen.

Almost Had It

As a jet of destruction streamed from Wand right at the wall, my intent to blast it through and let Mikalus be consumed by fire, Mikalus himself had other ideas.

"No," he screamed, and faster than I'd have believed possible he was on me. He tackled me and we rolled across the floor with him clawing at my face. I even lost my hat, and that really pissed me off.

My strike had gone wide, hitting not the wall but the ceiling, bringing down all kinds of crap into the room. Plasterboard, cabling, ducts, and pipework all clattered around us in a mess of thunder as metal struck metal and wires crackled dangerously. I was amazed the lights stayed on.

Mikalus was enraged for real now, a mindless creature, as if there was a shift like the Wild Ones and he was lost to the vampire. At the thought of the Wild Ones, I pictured Candy dead behind the counter in her tiny coffee shop and my anger surged.

"Get the fuck off me," I grunted, and as Mikalus tore at me I protected myself with a shield like invisible clothing. But the blows still pummeled me, and still forced me down lower from my position prone on my back with the manic form of a naked vampire over me, blood dripping from his mouth as he ripped at me and rained down blow after weighty blow.

I pushed back with a move of my own that I'd used way too often lately, a kick straight to the knackers, and even in his lost state the pain must have penetrated as he swore and lost his breath. In the pause I jabbed out hard with Wand, nothing magical, just an old favorite move, and Wand punctured Mikalus' eyeball with a satisfying pop.

"Ugh, gross," moaned Wand as I pulled him free with a sick sucking sound. But it didn't stop Mikalus and he smashed at me with both fists like a club to the head. The eye oozed and then it sealed shut before stickily opening moments later, staring and angry, weeping like a baby's as it sees for the first time and greets the world.

"You dare try to destroy me?" hissed Mikalus as he grabbed my arm. I think he was trying to pull it off.

I panicked. Maybe he would, he felt strong enough, and he yanked hard, almost tearing muscle.

"I just thought I'd redecorate," I mumbled, then let my will flow. Wand absorbed it like he was charging up, and without fanfare spat out a blackness that splatted against Mikalus' head then began to consume the space it occupied.

Mikalus howled and fell, then crawled backward across the floor as he batted at his face and screamed some more. He came up against a pile of ducting and used it to stand, then he breathed deep and roared, "I am the First."

My magic waned, the energy spent.

There were holes in his face, half his nose was gone, deep hollows that showed the insides of his head, and yet even that didn't stop him. My disappointment rose as the holes closed and pink raw flesh took its place.

Knowing I wasn't going to be able to fend him off a second time, I let Wand have free rein. He swung my arm at the wall then let rip once again.

This time he didn't miss, and our combined might blasted at the wall with every intention of opening it up to the lovely summer's day and burning away this annoyingly hard to kill vampire.

Nothing happened. Okay, plaster and brick and what have you exploded in a suitably impressive way, but it didn't reveal the day, it just revealed metal that glinted dully.

"Shit, he's got wards up," I said to nobody in particular.

"I'm not going to make the same mistake twice," said Mikalus with a grin. "You think I haven't thought about being attacked? Nothing can get through my defenses."

Mikalus stared at us hard, and then he smirked as his body cracked and things took a turn for the worrying.

Ugh, I hate smirkers. Well, at least I tried.

An Unexpected Twist

"Um, can you do that?" I asked, turning to Ivan so I could avoid looking at the freak show in front of us.

"I bloody hope not," said Ivan in disgust. He checked his own arms then the rest of his ruined upper body, as if expecting it to follow suit at any moment. I took a step away from him just in case, but all that happened was his body continued repairing itself.

"What about you?" I asked Carmichael, who came to join us, his black silk dressing gown still looking immaculate, which wasn't right or fair.

Carmichael shook his head, almost sadly, and I knew how he felt. "Only the First has such a curse. I read of this, was never sure if it was the truth or not. It's... this is..."

"Extreme? Worrying? A bit mad?"

Carmichael nodded, and the three of us stood, rather foolishly, but this had to be seen through to the end, in front of Mikalus as his metamorphosis continued.

I've seen all manner of peculiar beasties in my time. Some nice and cuddly looking, others not so much. I have summoned demons from the depths of the Nolands, have fought fae and battled insane things with way too many spikes and eyes that are molten lava. I have been sent to places that make Lovecraft's Cthulhu seem like a walk through a rainbow on the back of a unicorn, but this, this was worse because it was all too human.

Mikalus' change was almost complete now, and rather than hang around gawping any longer, I did what any sensible wizard would do under such circumstances and I took advantage while he couldn't fight back. As his bones broke and reconfigured, as his head stretched and his back sprouted demonic wings of a very un-fluffy kind, and strange things poked through his chest cavity and his knees bent in the wrong direction as the femurs grew to twice their regular length, I shunted my will into Wand and told him, "Destroy that thing."

"I'll give it a go, but I should warn you, it—"

I didn't wait for Wand to finish, just shoved hard with deadly intent. A radiant field of super-charged energy shot out then spread to envelop the monstrosity before me. Mikalus, or what was once Mikalus, howled in rage, then in what sounded like ecstasy as the magic hit then slid aside only to fizzle and die, like he was an aerodynamic plane able to slide through magic and remain undamaged.

And he grew, fast, which wasn't what I'd expected. He was absorbing magic and it was powering him up.

"What about that? Can you do that?"

"Alas, no," said Carmichael, watching in wonder at Mikalus' transformation.

Everyone has an image in their head of what a vampire really looks like, that they turn into something all skinny and bony with a hide like a bat and many other bat-like characteristics, all emaciated and hunched with leathery wings and sparkling deadly eyes set deep in a grotesque face. Hairless and covered with blemishes, that kind of thing. But vampires don't do that, they're just people, with power, and the need for blood to make them superhuman.

That's what I'd always told myself, what the vampires themselves knew to be true. Mikalus was clearly an exception. He looked unlike anything I'd ever seen before. His body was large, not skinny, like his skin had grown thick and hard like a rhino's, and all I could think of as I watched him grow was that he looked like a freaking T-Rex. That was it, he looked like a dinosaur. His head had lost most of the detail, mostly snout with two piggy eyes and tiny ears. The nostrils were huge, and he snorted loudly, but it was the teeth that drew your attention. Row after row of gleaming gnashers like something out of your worst nightmare. Just like a ferocious dinosaur.

His body was hunched forward, the vertebrae bent horribly, with a ridge of spines running up to the neck, getting larger and splitting skin as they fattened.

His arms were stunted things that waved almost ineffectively, tipped with curved talons.

His legs were huge though, fat tree trunks thick with muscle. The toes, or the blunt ends to what had been toes, were tipped with claws each as long as his feet. They gouged huge lines in the floor as Mikalus writhed about in agony, or ecstasy, it was hard to tell which.

A pair of tiny leathery wings protruded from his back, as if merely for show rather than any practical use. They beat frantically until they became a blur, and as the last remnants of my magic dissipated, all we were left with was this hybrid man-cum-rhino-cum-dinosaur-cum-vampire.

This was not what I'd come to learn vampires could be or were. Ivan certainly hadn't shared any of this when he told us about Mikalus and the history of their kind. But he'd been told that information by Mikalus, given permission to share with us, so it wasn't likely Mikalus would have offered such monstrous revelations. Maybe this was unique to him? I certainly hoped so.

Mikalus was the original, and who knew what went along with that? Clearly not Carmichael by the seems of it. Did Mikalus himself even know this was a possibility? Had it happened before?

The monster roared.

Time to Scarper

"Run?" I asked Ivan.
"Run," he agreed.
We ran.
And got nowhere.

Time to Think

The prehistoric beast, like a failed genetic experiment, lifted me up in one malformed hand and the talons closed tight around my middle. Ivan was grabbed in the other and I watched from on high as Carmichael ran for the door.

He didn't make it. Mikalus bellowed in rage and used Ivan like a misshapen bowling ball and threw him in Carmichael's direction. Ivan slid across the polished floor and slammed into Carmichael's legs, bowling him over. Thinking that I'd had a lucky escape as I watched Ivan crawl away, his arm at a most peculiar angle, I ran through a number of scenarios, trying to figure out how to destroy this monster. All the possibilities I could come up with didn't result in anything but a lot of squashed Hat, which was kind of depressing, so I did the only thing I could do, and tried to avoid getting bitten in two or eviscerated.

Mikalus turned beady eyes on me, sunken and myopic, that nonetheless could see me well enough up close. I could smell his foul breath, taste the sourness as he breathed in then snorted out, and then he snapped at me, the huge dinosaur head intent on taking my head off.

My hat went into overdrive, hard as Mikalus' ward-protected steel walls, and an umbrella of protection fanned out. It was handy in the rain, just as handy when attacked by prehistoric beasties. I felt the reverberation through the creature's body as its teeth shattered against Grace, but it didn't pause, just snapped over and over, pile-driving me so it felt like my neck was about to break or I'd at least be several inches shorter when this was all over.

Ha, when this was all over. Even now, The Hat had confidence he'd get out of this alive, and that meant there was a plan somewhere in my feeble mind, a way to beat this even though I couldn't imagine what it was.

Then Mikalus tried a different approach. He pulled his spindly arm back and with inhuman force he threw me right at the wall. I hit hard, side-on, and landed just as badly. The wards flared on the wall angrily, keeping the integrity of the steel intact, but it sparked something in my mind and I finally had a plan.

Wasting no time, and as Mikalus advanced on Ivan and Carmichael who were hurriedly trying to get up and away somehow, I focused Wand on the wall and ran through numerous ancient spells and devious ways to negate wards.

"That won't work," said Wand.

"Why not?"

"Because your spells are out of date. This is modern stuff, just for a specific purpose, and besides, they're impenetrable. These wards are here to stay."

"Ah, right," I said, panicked. "Um, any ideas?"

"Yeah, course. We're a team. Leave it to me."

I shrugged, like I had a choice.

Wand spun in my hand even as I regained my feet, and he spat a spear of white pain that lanced the monster's foot, or it should have, but Mikalus' appendage merely hardened and the talons grew more fearful.

"That's not a good plan," I noted.

"You'll see."

Mikalus roared his annoyance and changed direction, moving fast to me, arms clawing the air.

"And this is helpful how?"

"Just wait, but don't forget to dodge."

"Eh, what? What's the plan?"

No time, as Mikalus was almost upon me. As a hind leg kicked out with incredible speed, the talons capable of tearing me in two, I sidestepped just in time and the deadly foot connected with the wall. Metal screeched, the talons clawed down fast and hard, and left a deep gouge in the steel.

With that, the wards burned brightly then died. Mikalus had taken them down himself, the only one who could. His actions had somehow negated the wards, which meant I could attack the steel and burn a damn hole right through.

I ran around behind him and Wand was lifted high. Feeling euphoric, I summoned as much of my will as remained and focused on a spot on the wall, ready to blast this puppy back to the stone age. And just as my sigils flared, the damn wards popped back into place, red and angry and stronger than ever.

"Some fucking plan," I moaned.

Wand had the good grace to remain quiet.

An Aha Moment

Mikalus spun on his not inconsiderable heels, his rear claws piercing the floor like it was sponge and pulling away the remains of the skirting board. Ivan and Carmichael dashed over. Ivan said, "We have to get out of here. Let's go," and looked at me hopefully.

"Why don't you blast the door, or just open it?" I asked Carmichael, who was looking at me like Ivan was. As if I had the answers to this.

"Because of him. We can't leave until this is settled. Look at him. You are seeing what I'm seeing, right?"

"Yeah, I'm seeing it," I sighed, but why they both thought I could deal with this when these two were vampires and I knew for a fact Carmichael had deep magical ability of his own, I didn't know. Then I got it.

"You can't use magic at the moment, can you?"

"No, and don't ask me why," snapped Carmichael, looking stressed for the first time.

"Why?" I asked. You would, right?

Carmichael sighed, pulled the dressing gown tighter as we all kept a careful eye on the thing that was Mikalus as he snorted and roared and generally trashed the floor as he watched us with hate in his eyes.

"Because I haven't had time to go to the Quiet Place. I'm wiped out. You have no idea the trouble all this has caused, the things I've had to do to get the warehouse moved. It was exhausting. Then," he said, pointing at me, "you blew me up, set me on fire, took my life's work, and brought me here."

"Blimey, don't get shirty. This is all your fault anyway."

"If we can save the bickering for later?" said Ivan as he flung himself aside and a foot the size of a, well, the size of a T-Rex's foot, crashed down and punched an impressive hole in the floor.

"Good idea," I shouted as I ran away.

I hid behind Mikalus who was now utterly out of control. People began to bang at the door to the penthouse; they'd be through in minutes. This wasn't going to get easier, it was going to get a lot harder.

I backed up against the steel and felt the power of the wards encompassing the length of the outer wall, and stared down morosely at my boots. Something caught my eye, a view down to the apartment below, and then, as if by divine intervention, although I knew He wouldn't lift a finger to help this poor wizard, I had an epiphany.

"I bet they didn't bother," I muttered, and with that I stepped away from the wall, spun to face it, and lifted Wand as Mikalus grabbed Carmichael and manhandled him to his mouth.

"This is more like it," said Wand with glee. "An actual plan."

"Just blast it good, real good," I ordered.

Wand spasmed into life like a fireman's hose spouting magic. Great thick streams of sparkling heat erupted from his tip and chewed up the floor against the wall as I carefully moved my arm from left to right, taking out the floor in a rough line. Girders and wooden joists were revealed, the supports for the building and for the floor itself. I saw what I was interested in, a girder that ran along the outer wall, installed to hold the steel that acted as Mikalus' protection against the sun.

With grim determination, I gritted my teeth and pushed Wand to his limits, and mine, and aimed at the center of the beam. It was unprotected, just regular steel, and was melted through in a moment.

Carmichael screamed, his face inches from Mikalus' jaws, but he was on his own for now. Ivan ran to the door, yanked it open, fired rapidly, then slammed it shut and ran back to me.

"Why didn't you use the gun on Mikalus?" I bellowed above the roar of Mikalus, the splintering wood, and a groan that became louder and louder.

"Because he's a vampire. Duh." Ivan actually smiled, guess he was trying to be funny.

"Okay, get ready."

"For what?"

"For some sunbathing."

The girder lost it's seating on either side and fell down into the suite below. As it dropped, so the massive sheet of steel welded to span the whole wall slipped a little then caught on the original supports.

"Shit," I squealed, but then a sliver of light appeared right where the wall met the ceiling, and I turned at the ungodly screams coming from behind.

The raised arm of Mikalus, still holding Carmichael, was ablaze, burning with an intensity I'd never witnessed before. It was brighter than any magic, more violent than any conflagration I'd caused, and hotter than hell itself. I could feel it on my face, feel my hair singeing. The pain must have been unbearable.

Mikalus screamed until his throat was raw as his arm spasmed, the hand clutching tighter until I thought Carmichael would pop. He was screaming too, hardly surprising as inches of hard keratin pierced his flesh.

Then with a whoosh the flame intensified as the sun shone brighter and Carmichael was released. He scrambled away, body torn and strips of flesh hanging, but he didn't stop until he was against a wall.

Mikalus lowered his arm but as he did so it disintegrated, turned to ash and fell to the floor.

I checked the steel hurriedly, not wanting to take my eyes off Mikalus. The wards were down, gone for good.

"Your time to shine, mate," I whispered to Wand, who nodded, which was weird, and let loose with a concentrated stream of increasingly impotent magic as our power died, drained from us.

The steel melted through easily. First a small hole, which made Mikalus scramble to get out of the way of the sunlight, then it spread until a gaping hole from floor to ceiling gave a magnificent view out over this city where so many good days, and many more worse ones, had been had.

Spent, I pocketed Wand with a silent thank you. I felt his presence dwindle as if he too was exhausted and had to sleep. Then he was silent.

But the room wasn't.

The beast went wild.

This wasn't over.

Uncaged

Mikalus roared in utter anguish as he stared myopically at his stub of an arm. As light streamed in high in the room, the impossible creature bent its head and went apoplectic with rage. He dropped low on his legs and charged around the room wildly, tail whacking against walls, thudding against the floor so hard it broke the boards—I'd forgotten about the tail.

He raced past the opening, his body steaming as he caught the daylight, but as soon as he reached a darker place he began to heal, but not the arm. How could he continue in such a state? How was it possible? My mind reeled with the agony he must be experiencing as his skin erupted time after time only to be doused moments later as this primordial force he contained sought to protect its host. This was true otherworldly magic and I could only think that maybe his resurrection had strengthened him against the dangers he faced by sunlight.

Would he manage to get out of this alive? That was unthinkable, as we'd all be hunted down no matter the cost. We remained motionless, watching from in front of the huge gap in the wall as Mikalus tore around the room, burning then healing then burning. He crouched, he flung himself against walls, he rolled on the floor, and each time he recovered a little more of him was lost. There were chunks missing from his body now, huge bits vanished as though they'd never been. Like bites had been taken out of him by an invisible monster more terrifying than himself.

And then the sun peeked from behind two skyscrapers, shining directly into the room in a small sliver.

"Move out the way," I ordered. Carmichael and Ivan stared at me with blank expressions. "You're blocking the light," I said softly as I turned and nodded at the sun as it blinded me.

They moved, as did I, and it was almost like trumpets blew as the room became awash with golden light.

Mikalus' strange body was transformed in an instant as true sunlight hit his ruined flesh. He visibly shrank, joints popped, and he returned to being a man, but a broken one.

He crumpled to the floor, moaning and whimpering, curled up tight, naked and alone, terrified and unable to bear the pain. With a scream that still haunts me, his flesh burst into flame for a single instant before the fire died, revealing the shape of an ash man, gray and lifeless.

Then the illusion was gone, and the ash fell to the floor in a heap. All that remained of the First.

Mikalus was dead.
Again.

Time to Reflect

We stood either side of a gaping hole at the top of vampire headquarters, staring in mute astonishment at the pile of ash on the floor. Had any of that happened? It was hard to believe it had. Was Mikalus really dead? Was that good, or very, very bad?

Probably bad, as what now?

Not my problem, it was theirs. They'd managed for hundreds of years without him, I'm sure they'd cope now he was gone again. Back to their secret ways, staying under the radar of the magical community as they always had, secretly working their way toward a future vision they didn't feel fit to share with the rest of us.

I turned to Ivan, about to say something but thought better of it as I saw a single tear fall. I understood. I really did.

He'd loved that man, been welcomed into a family that spread around the globe, each of them having something undeniable in common, each in part owing their existence to Mikalus. And he'd been betrayed by him. Used, abused, sold out. Ivan had experienced all of that, and more, before, and it broke my heart to see him trying to cope with such a betrayal of his love and trust.

He could have maybe accepted it all, found a way to deal with it, as he and I both knew that people were cruel, and none could hurt you more than those you loved.

It was Vicky that had been the real blow, that Mikalus would try to take that away from him. True family, a blood bond he cherished and would lay down his life for. That had to hurt more than all the rest combined.

"It's done," I whispered, putting an arm around my friend. Yes, I thought of him as that. Nothing like fighting tyrannical overlords to make two blokes buddies. I felt I could finally trust him, and maybe he felt the same way, as he turned and smiled.

"How very touching," said Carmichael, a fake smile plastered on his entirely smackable face.

"Shut up, we're having a moment."

"Maybe you could do that later, after the noise is dealt with?"

It took a moment for me to register what he was talking about, but I focused and could hear the clamoring the other side of the door. More vampire goons had come to the rescue, I assumed. With a sigh, I pulled Wand from my pocket and, thinking it best not to show Carmichael that I talked to it, I spoke silently in my mind. "You up for this?"

Wand took several seconds to stir, as if deep in slumber, the lucky bugger, then he sparked into life and I heard his voice in my head. "Sure, but then I must rest."

Wand spasmed in my hand and shot out seven narrow lines of red fire like a laser. Six penetrated the wall, one went through the door, and then there were no more shouts.

"Nice shooting," I congratulated, but he was already gone, back to wherever it was sentient Wands went when they slept. "Sweet dreams, my friend."

I turned to Carmichael. "There, that should buy us a few minutes. And don't even think about it," I warned as I caught him staring at the mounds of books, most of which were still intact, if rather bruised where they'd been knocked off the shelves.

"Wouldn't dream of it, my dear fellow."

"Shut up," I sighed.

"Your call," I said to Ivan.

He nodded, then walked over to a pile of ash and bent down.

Would he box up Mikalus and when he felt the world was ready allow the First to be resurrected once more?

Guess I'd find out soon enough.

It All Sucks

"Never again," said Ivan as he bent down and scooped up the ashes of the first true vampire in his shaking, cupped palms. Slowly, almost reverentially, he walked back to the edge of the destroyed wall. I stepped forward, knowing Carmichael wasn't about to push us out to our death, and went and stood by Ivan's side.

Carmichael joined us, returned from inspecting the books I would make damn sure he never, ever got to put in his warehouse, and the three of us stared out into the decaying city. Tall spires shone, office blocks gleamed. Cranes and scaffolding-covered buildings either half-constructed or in need of repair littered the city, as if it was crying out for peace, to be left to die with dignity rather than this expensive and prolonged fight against the inevitable it was suffering. Everything was always changing; more incredibly expensive modern architectural blights being built even as the old were abandoned. What were these people thinking? Couldn't they see what I saw?

As I scanned the city, I saw the truth in the distance in every direction. A foulness like a cancer spreading, creeping toward the center. Decaying buildings, abandoned warehouses, tenements ready for demolition. Cracked pavements and pot-holed roads. Dilapidated terraces where the tenants huddled around gas fires in the winter for warmth and sweltered in their boxes during this heatwave as the noxious air silently choked everyone to death.

The marshlands cleared to provide more land to build more homes on to accommodate the pressing need for affordable housing was already reclaiming what was lost. They never did build the houses. I caught glimpses of the canals and the rivers that broke their banks each year and washed away mankind's best efforts. The myriad roads criss-crossing above the stinking outer limits of the city, bypassing the degradation and the filth, pretending it wasn't down there in the mud, an inevitable future most refused to accept or even acknowledge.

But it was spreading, this decay, and it was coming for them all. A darkness was descending. The rich were getting richer, the poor were getting poorer, and every day more people lost hope, failed to find a way in this modern world. One day it would all come to a head and these clinical wonders reaching for the sky as if to get away from the very land they were built on would topple, and with it civilization.

For now, we were all still struggling down in the mire, trying to make the best of things, but when you looked, when you really looked, you could see it coming, see the end encroaching. Soon enough it would claim us all.

Ivan stepped forward to the edge and peered down. He put his arms out in front of him and waited.

A gust of wind eddied around us, then howled out from behind as it hit the rear wall then bounced back, pushing at us. Ivan opened his hands.

Ash scattered to the wind as the sun disappeared behind a futile monument to the hopes and dreams of humanity.

Equestrian Bliss

"You sure you don't want a lesson?" asked George as she trotted past me on a horse darker than Death's Sunday best and a lot more menacing.

"No thanks. I like my bones where they are," I said, glaring at the horse as it snorted at me in contempt, a blast of warm air thick in the icy morning.

George smiled and waved as she geed the well-muscled horse up and they continued their exercise around the new training school, the thick sand we'd had laid making it unlikely, but inevitable in my case, to break bones if you fell off.

The terrible twosome shouted and hollered with glee as they hung on for dear life and cajoled their horses to speed up as they chased after George.

I put my arm around Vicky's shoulder and smiled down at her. She was grinning like the madwoman she was, pleased as punch to see her children so happy.

A lot had happened in the months it eventually took to purchase the new property, solicitors and estate agents managing to drag it out for ages, wickedly and perversely determined to do so. But we moved in despite the evil men in cheap suits. Me and George settled in a new farm, a massive house with the most awesome kitchen in the known universe, and her equestrian business was set up.

Vicky and the girls moved from their mansion to something more manageable in the city, and they were happier because of it. They came down to visit most weekends, the girls having been shown the wonders of the Gates of Bakaudif then sworn to secrecy. They loved it, loved all things magical, and I worried about their future. But there was plenty of time to stress about that. For now, they were just kids having the never-ending adventure of a lifetime.

"Don't get any funny ideas," warned Vicky, glancing at my hand on her shoulder.

"Wouldn't dream of it," I said with a grin, knowing we were well past that, would never return.

I jumped back as George came around again and the horse whinnied, much to everyone else's amusement. Vicky took my arm and put hers through it and we walked away from the arena, staring at the newly refurbished farmhouse.

"How are you doing?" she asked, staring up at me with her big brown eyes.

"Fine," I shrugged.

"Arthur, I mean how are you really? You don't have to lie."

"Vicky, if I admitted to you, or myself, how I really feel, then I'd go find a very sharp knife and slit my wrists."

"That bad, eh?"

"Worse. I'm not good. I'm hanging in there, but I feel betrayed and useless, and so sad inside it aches. I thought I'd found a future with Candy, and look what happened. I disgust myself and people disgust me in return for what they're capable of. Me included."

"But you've got me," she said, smiling, and beginning to... No, she wouldn't.

"Don't you dare," I warned, panic setting in.

"You love it." It was too late, Vicky released her hold on me and began the most awful thing in the known universe. The Vicky mom-dance.

Her hips gyrated in a way mortifying to all of humanity, she began to do disgusting things with her arms, and then she put the nail in the coffin of all things unholy by tilting her head back and doing this weird thing with her mouth that made a terrifying noise come out between her stupid lips. She called it singing, but she must have a dictionary with a very different definition of it to me.

I had to laugh, otherwise I'd cry. Vicky knew me so well, knew how to break my depression. Without her I don't know if I'd have made it through, as I would have gone off on a mad one, more reckless than ever, and got myself killed over and over until the game was up. As it was, after the madness with Cerberus and the vampires, things settled down for me and my family.

The same couldn't be said for the vampires. Ivan's actions had sent a shockwave through the community that was still being felt.

Ah, screw it, that was their problem. I had all I needed right here. So I grabbed Vicky's hands and I danced in a freezing cold field on a winter's morning and you know what? I think I actually felt happy.

Just for a while.

The End

Book 6, Lost Hope, coming soon.

Get author updates and new release notifications first via the Newsletter.

Read the Dark Magic Enforcer series for more magical mayhem.

Printed in Great Britain
by Amazon

44650730R00196